Emma H. Adams

**Savonarola**

The Florentine martyr

Emma H. Adams

**Savonarola**
*The Florentine martyr*

ISBN/EAN: 9783337314194

Printed in Europe, USA, Canada, Australia, Japan

Cover: Foto ©Andreas Hilbeck / pixelio.de

More available books at **www.hansebooks.com**

Fra Girolamo Savonarola.

# THE FLORENTINE MARTYR

By EMMA H. ADAMS

AUTHOR OF "FIJI AND SAMOA," "TO AND FRO IN SOUTHERN CALI-
FORNIA," "UP AND DOWN IN OREGON AND WASHINGTON."

PACIFIC PRESS PUBLISHING COMPANY
OAKLAND, CAL.
SAN FRANCISCO, NEW YORK, AND LONDON

# CONTENTS.

( v )

## CHAPTER XI.

## CHAPTER XII.

## CHAPTER XIII.

## CHAPTER XIV.

## CHAPTER XV.

## CHAPTER XVI.

## CHAPTER XVII.

## CHAPTER XVIII.

## CHAPTER XIX.

## CHAPTER XX.

## CHAPTER XXI.

## CHAPTER XXII.

## CHAPTER XXIII.

# SAVONAROLA,

## THE FLORENTINE MARTYR.

## CHAPTER I.

### THE MIDDLE OF THE FIFTEENTH CENTURY.

 ANY a time in human history has a brilliant dawn been preceded by a "dark hour," gloomier than the midnight,—an hour when scarcely a star beamed through the dense fog of evil which enwrapped the world; when hardly a voice could be heard as the harbinger of the coming day; when, in State affairs, in religious concerns, in social life, sin had so paralyzed the conscience of mankind that the statement of the great apostle had become almost literally true: "They are all gone out of the way. . . There is none that doeth good. . . The poison of asps is under their lips. . . . Their feet are swift to shed blood."

Sometimes at such gloomy periods the fog has

(7)

suddenly drifted away, or the clouds have parted
for a moment, and through the rift the light of a
radiant star has illumined the earth for a short time,
but only to render the darkness more apparent.

Emphatically, such an hour of darkness was the
middle of the fifteenth century.   It was the dreary,
melancholy closing of the long night of the Dark
Ages, during which professed Christianity held the
corrupting hand of heathenism, and the two walked
amicably together—*really one.*

And, emphatically, such a lustrous star, shining
but for a moment of years through the temporarily-
parted clouds, was Girolamo Savonarola, the subject
of this sketch.

Nevertheless, in some respects that hour of deep
moral gloom was an era of unsurpassed glory and
magnificence.   It was a day of splendid triumphs
in art, of illustrious achievements in scholarship, of
amazing displays of wealth and power on the part
of the church,—such display as only a corrupt
church, closely allied to a corrupt state, could
exhibit.   It was not the setting forth of brotherly
love, of tender patience, of the peerless truth, all
through grace divine.   Princes and prelates vied
with each other in oppressing the people.   Both
heartlessly robbed them.   Both kept them quiet
and uncomplaining with spectacles and amusements, while they did so.   The money wrung
from them painted the immortal pictures, chiseled
the enduring sculptures, filled the great libraries,
reared the noble churches.

This dark hour symbolizes the reigns of the Popes
Sixtus IV., Innocent VIII., and Alexander VI., at
Rome—the rallying-point for all the wily priest-
craft of the earth ; and the rule of Cosmo, Lorenzo,
and Pietro de Medici, at Florence—then the center
of art and learning in Italy. Of that era one has
remarked: " Italy, then, was the most corrupt portion of christendom." Another has added: " The
external garb of society was elegance. The condition of its heart was rottenness."

It was the day of Bartolommeo, foremost of
Florentine painters ; of Baldini, the inimitable illus-
trator of Dante ; of Michael Angelo, in whom
painting, sculpture, and architecture were almost
personified, and who "chiseled marble furiously,"
during the very days, when Savonarola, using the
sword of truth, endeavored to shape anew the
hearts of the Florentine multitude.

Most inaptly was that period called " The Era of
the New Learning," or " The New Birth of Learning;" for in fact the mightiest efforts of all its men of
genius were put forth, only to infuse new life into
the old paganism, and to render its glory the more
effulgent by robing it in the dress of Christianity.
The " new learning" was simply greater devotion to
pagan authors and artists, and an intensified desire
to make larger collections of their works.

At the same time, unhappily, it was an age when
lords and kings made much of the church. All
espoused her cause; all wanted to live within her

pale. But they were there, as men dead in tres-
passes and sins, hardly with names to live. Virtu-
ally, they were heathen. To escape the scourgings
of conscience, they flatly denied what the word of
God so clearly asserts, a judgment after death. Of
all this, what was the outcome?—Just what we
should expect,—men, professing to be the children
of God, in order to secure the power, the position,
the wealth, they coveted, committed the most atro-
cious crimes. Not long did lordly nobles, or even
titled priests, hesitate over the sacrificing of a human
life, which intervened between themselves and ends
they desired.

Thus, it was at an epoch when the titled classes
had reached the extreme of greed and rapacity, and
when the humble ranks were benumbed through
spoliation and repression, that Savonarola stepped
upon the scene, like a shining figure out of the
black night, holding aloft for a moment the blazing
torch of truth, and loudly warning all who said,
"God doth not see," that vengeance was drawing
nigh; and that done, suddenly extinguishing his
torch and withdrawing into the night.

But who was Savonarola?

In the gay city of Ferrara, the capital of a province of that name, in Italy, on September 21, 1452,
was born Girolamo Savonarola, just thirty years
before the birth of Martin Luther. But let us,
before entering upon his life and work, acquaint
ourselves with the once illustrious city in which

Savonarola spent the first twenty-three years of his life.

About the beginning of the thirteenth century, the city and province of Ferrara became the possession of the powerful Esté family, which retained control of it until 1495—three years before the death of its famous citizen, Savonarola. During the last century of the Esté government, Ferrara contained one of the most cultured courts in all Italy. Its name will be forever associated with much that was purest and best in Italian literature. In a street of Ferrara, still bearing his name, stands the house in which dwelt the poet Ariosto. The famous poet Tasso wrote and was imprisoned there. Other distinguished authors first drew breath in the proud little capital. Some of the princes of Esté were generous patrons of learning. In 1498, Pope Alexander VI. included the province of Ferrara in the papal States.

In the very center of the city—its population one hundred thousand—is located the old ducal palace. It is surrounded by a deep moat, and crowned by frowning battlements.

Anciently, Savonarola's family lived in Padua; but about 1440, his grandfather, Michele Savonarola, removed to Ferrara, being invited thither by the third prince of Esté, who was distinguished as a patron of literature and the arts. Nicholas, a son of Michele, was the father of Girolamo Savonarola, one of the most gifted, and to-day one of the most eminent, characters in Italian history.

His mother, Helena Anna Buonaccossi, was from a notable old Paduan family, and was a woman of strong character, of kindly heart, and was devoted to her famous son. In all the dark and terrible hours of his life, she was his unfailing comfort. Many letters still extant evince the tender love existing between mother and son.

Authentic details of Savonarola's boyhood are scanty, and are of little interest. He is represented as having been a reserved and serious youth, not fond of amusements, but delighting in solitude and charmed with learning. As a boy he loved to wander along the banks of the Po, reading Arab comments upon Aristotle, and the works of Thomas Aquinas, a Dominican theologian of remarkable philosophical attainments.

To a degree quite beyond his age, the young Girolamo understood the subtle reasonings of the schools. His grandfather, a physician of rare understanding, guided the boy's early reading, but quite in the line of his own profession, as the highest hope of his parents, with reference to his temporal good, was to see him adorn the pursuit of his grandfather, who, both in Padua and Ferrara, had become eminent as a physician and as a professor of physical science. But he died—at the age of seventy-nine—while as yet Girolamo had made little progress, and left him to the tuition of his father, who appears to have been really unequal to the task.

The boy had now arrived at the age of ten, and was a pupil in the public schools of Ferrara.  In that day the study of Aristotle and the works of Thomas Aquinas was considered a necessary preparation for any profession.  And soon the lad was master of them.  Aquinas was his favorite, and day after day was whiled away in meditation upon his teachings.

Thomas Aquinas, or Thomas of Aquino, was born about 1226, and  died March 4, 1274, at the early age of forty-eight.

The highest honors the Catholic Church could bestow were accorded to his memory.  Pope John XXII. placed his name in the calendar of the saints.  Thomas Aquinas has been designated as "the spirit of scholasticism incarnate."  Of his age —decidedly one of subtle study rather than one of active Christian work—he was its blazing, central star.

# CHAPTER II.

HIS man, then, was the entrancing author upon whose speculations and reasonings young Savonarola fed daily. So absorbed in them did he become that he turned with great difficulty to other more important studies. Nevertheless, to live the truth in its purity, for its own sake, was even then his highest aim. "Young as he was," writes one, "he turned in disdain from writers who, in the *name* of truth, set forth only their own opinions." Such books he was accustomed to lay aside with the remark, "They do not please me." Thus was formed a habit of close study and of careful reasoning upon a subject which, in after years, was of exceeding value to him, particularly when obliged to discuss difficult and controverted points with men of trained minds.

Yet the day came when Savonarola looked back upon the years he had devoted to that sort of study as time thrown away. Referring to the subject after his mind had become illumined by the word of God, he was heard to say:—

"I was then in the error of the schools. I studied with great assiduity the dialogues of Plato. But

(14)

when God brought me to see the true light, I cast
them away.  Of what avail is Plato," he would
ask, " when a poor woman, established in the faith
of Christ, knows more of true wisdom than does
he ? "

There was little promise that young Savonarola
would adopt the arduous, practical life of a physician, when he constantly turned away from the studies needful to the profession.  And we are not surprised to find that, as time rolled on, there sprang
up a vehement conflict between his own inclinations
and the wishes of his parents; nor that very soon
he abandoned all thought of thus spending his life.
But to what vocation would he turn instead?  We
shall see.

Savonarola was far from being an ascetic.  He
was capable of great devotion to a friend.  His
heart beat in warm sympathy for those around him,
particularly for the oppressed.  And very painful
to him was the collision between his own tastes
and the plan of his parents for him.  But more and
more, on account of its wickedness, did the world
become repulsive to him.  He possessed an innate
love of purity, and was painfully alive to the corruption of the age.

The Palace of Esté, always a delightful resort for
the merry citizens of Ferrara, held out no attrac-
tions for the youth.  Once, in company with his parents, he had joined the throng there; had walked
through its splendid saloons, while he knew that

underneath, in dismal dungeons, lay human beings
living out years of death.  Above, could be heard
the voices of music and laughter; below, the clank-
ing of chains and the groans of the tortured.  The
effect of his reflections upon this condition of things
was most dispiriting.  "Sad and weary he left the
gay halls to weep alone over the misery he could
neither end nor alleviate."  His parents could never
again induce him to pay the Palace of Esté a visit.

About this time, perhaps, or when about nine-
teen, there occurred an event which, added to
many other considerations, must have hastened his
conclusion as to how his life should be spent.  In
the neighborhood of his home, there resided a family by the name of Strozzi, exiles from the city of
Florence.  To a daughter of the household he became ardently attached.  But, upon declaring his
regard, he was disdainfully informed that no Strozzi
would condescend to marry a Savonarola.  Bitterly
did he resent the affront.  He had believed her to
be a true woman.  But he had learned otherwise.
His disappointment was in time overbalanced by a
sense of her demerit.

Two years passed away now, years of misery
and mental conflict.  The period was one of keen
self-distrust.  He could not feel that either his unhappy disappointment or his dislike of the hypo-
critical world were genuine qualifications for a religious life.  What, therefore, was he to do?  Into
what path should he turn?  Who would help him

to decide? Fortunately, he turned to the right
source for help. His constant prayer now was,
" Lord, teach me the way my soul should walk!"

Savonarola now diligently studied his Bible, together with his beloved Aquinas, and "for recrea-
tion," says one biographer, "played mournful airs
on the lute, and wrote verses in which he poured
forth the sorrows of his heart." For example, in
his poem entitled "De Ruina Mundi"—"The Destruction of the World"—written in 1472, he thus
laments :—

" The whole world is in confusion ; every virtue
has disappeared ; no shining light is to be seen ;
none are ashamed of their sins. Had it not been
for my confidence in the overruling providence of
God, I should have been driven to despair by the
aspect of affairs." The sight of " scepters passing
into the hands of pirates, of Religion turning her
face earthwards and crawling amid earthly loves
and cares," was more than he could bear.

It was about the same period that he wrote:
" There is still a hope which does not entirely
abandon me : that is, that in the other life it will
be clearly seen whose soul was gentle and kind,
and who elevated his wings to a higher style." By
this " higher style " did he mean a religious life in
a monastery? a life which now began to appear to
the devout student—as it did not very long after to
Martin Luther—the very gate of heaven ? asks one
who wrote without prejudice of Savonarola.

2

Day by day, life in a cloister seems to have gained upon his regard, though he never mentioned the subject to his parents, understanding perfectly how serious would be their objection to it. But conscience urged it. In no other way—in the Italy of that period—did it appear possible to devote himself to the service of God and the welfare of his fellow-men. Thus did young Savonarola reason. And not long after, a sermon preached by an Augustinian monk enabled him to settle the matter beyond reversion. He listened to this sermon in Florence, in 1474, and appears to have accepted what he heard as the answer to his oft-repeated prayer, "O Lord, teach me the way my soul should walk!" It was but a "single word" he afterward said, which decided him, but what that single word was he never divulged.

Harassed no longer now by indecision as to his vocation, Girolamo returned to Ferrara. But as he approached his home, he was overwhelmed with sadness at the prospect of leaving it forever. Parents, friends, everything he held dear, thronged his soul. Thereafter for days followed a mighty contest between the flesh and the spirit. In vain did he try to conceal his trouble. The quick eye of his mother detected grief which had not been confided to her, and which for that reason was all the more difficult to bear. Never before had he hidden from her a single joy or sorrow. And now her look of tender questioning he could not endure, and dared not trust himself to meet again. Therefore, for an entire year the young man so controlled himself as not for a moment to recall that irresistible look from his mother.

Long afterward he said, speaking of that struggle: " Had I then laid open my whole mind to my mother, I believe my heart would have broken. I should have renounced my intention of becoming a monk."

On the 24th of April, 1475, Girolamo's life in the home of his boyhood came to an end. The evening preceding, while sitting beside his mother, playing melancholy strains on the lute, she suddenly exclaimed, "My son, this means that we are soon to part!" Appearing as though he heard her not, Savonarola continued to play, but with a trembling hand, and without lifting his eyes to her face. Next day there occurred a great holiday in Ferrara—the festival of St. George. Immediately after his parents left the house to attend the ceremonies, Savonarola bade the place a silent adieu and departed for Bologna. He was then twenty-three years of age.

His exalted regard for Thomas Aquinas, "the glory of the Dominican order," induced Savonarola to become a Dominican monk. Consequently, upon arriving at Bologna, he went directly to the Monastery of St. Dominic. Feeling that the most menial office within its walls was better than he deserved, he prayed to be admitted simply as a servant, that he might in that capacity "do penance for his sins "—nor was it with the expectation then

so usual in the minds of men entering such institutions, of soon passing from the secular occupations
of the place, to the more congenial ones of the
cloister.

Having now taken the important step—how important he then but faintly conceived—Girolamo
was confronted by a most painful duty. He must
write his father and mother and account for his
sudden flight. He realized profoundly that his
absence had filled their home with sorrow. To
explain his leaving was an easy matter. But how
could he justify it? How could he comfort the
heart of his mother, so strongly bound to him?
One thing he *could* do. He could acknowledge
that his own pain at parting from them had been
grievously acute. Besides, he could write with
absolute candor as to his motives. So, the first
night, before he laid himself down upon his com-
fortless pallet, he wrote his parents with all the tenderness of his loving heart, "not wishing another
sun to rise upon the home he had left forever"
until he had done what he could to mitigate the
grief therein.

In this letter he made no attempt to justify his
course, but rather endeavored to lead his parents to
take a lofty view of the life before him, of its peace
and usefulness. He says: "My hope is that the
wounds will soon heal and be followed, even in this
world, by the consolation of God's grace, and in the
next, by glory." The letter bore the date, Bologna,
April 25, 1475. In it Savonarola referred to a tract

which his father " would find upon the books in the
window."

Its title was "The Wickedness of the Times,"
which he claimed were like those of Sodom and
Gomorrah. And in it, as if to him the veil of the
future were already drawn aside, he said: " But
already we see signs of famine, and pestilence, and
inundations, which will proclaim God's wrath."
Then he implores: " Part again, O Lord, the waters
of the Red Sea, and drown the wicked in the waves
of thine indignation!"

His father found the tract, and upon it penciled
these sad but cutting lines : " I remember how, on
the 24th day of April, which was St. George's Day,
in the year 1475, my son Girolamo, then a student
of arts, being intended for the medical profession,
left our house, went to Bologna, and entered the
Dominican Convent, intending to remain there and
become a monk; leaving me, Michele Savonarola,
nothing but these writings." These lines paint in
most vivid colors the icy desolation of the father's
heart. No end of similar trials, and countless
greater ones, have been caused by the monastic institutions of Rome.

Until recently this tract was believed to be lost.
It is considered valuable, because, from the very
dawn of his distinctively religious life, Savonarola
believed he saw severe judgments impending over
Italy. And it also faintly hints the hope that to
him might be committed the noble mission of reforming the shockingly backslidden church.

# CHAPTER III.

ET us follow Savonarola to the monastery at Bologna, that we may learn how men who have voluntarily renounced the world in which God has placed them, in order to live lives of special sanctity and good works. Here, as in many situations, we shall discover that some things are not as attractive as they seem.

Savonarola entered the convent at Bologna, accompanied by one Ludovico, a young member of the order, to whom had been intrusted the secret of his flight. The monks welcomed him cordially, and although he came making no pretensions, the superior soon discovered his qualifications, and almost immediately appointed him instructor of the classes in philosophy and physics. Savonarola accepted the office with regret. But he regarded prompt obedience as a prime evidence of true spiritual life, and so at once yielded to the call of duty, and thereafter, with unflagging energy, labored for his pupils.

A sketch of Savonarola's manners and personal appearance at this time will help us to better under-

(22)

stand the impression he made at twenty-three. He was of medium height, of dark complexion; had luminous brown eyes, which sparkled and flamed under heavy black brows; had a large mouth and prominent under lip, which could express great tenderness, or wonderful power and determination. As a whole, his face, though thin, was rendered beautiful by a singular expression of benevolence and gentleness, which it ever wore. In manners he was very simple and natural. His speech, unadorned and almost rude, gave no hint of the splendid oratorical power which slumbered within him. He possessed an extremely delicate nervous system and "a temperament almost always allied to genius." It is said there is not a portrait of the man in existence that is not extremely ugly.

Girolamo's main authorities in teaching were his beloved Aquinas, St. Augustine, and the Holy Scriptures. The latter he had to an unprecedented degree committed to memory. Of the Old Testament prophets and the book of Revelation he was extremely fond. To have studied the Bible with the young men in his charge, and through belief in its truths have led them to God, would have been his delight. Like Wycliffe at Oxford, years before, he found his pupils utterly ignorant of God, and that they infinitely preferred Aristotle to the Scriptures. Moreover, he was compelled, as he said, to devote hours daily "to lecturing upon mere vanities."

As a first step upon entering the convent, Savonarola received the habit of the order, and a change
of name. His full name being Girolamo Maria
Francesco, the prior withdrew merely the two middle names, leaving the first to recall the memory of
the early church father, Jerome. From the day
he entered upon the new life, the young monk rig-
idly kept the three vows of the order—chastity,
obedience, and poverty. So correct was he in every
respect that the eminent ecclesiastic, Sebastiano da
Brescia, who was for many years Savonarola's confessor, declared that he believed he had never committed any marked sin. His simple, unfeigned
humility toward his brethren—a rare virtue in the
convent—drew all hearts.

Outside of his class-room, where oftentimes his
manner was so fervid that his pupils were awe-
struck, he conversed but little; yet when he did
speak, his words, flowing from a heart full of love
toward God and man, charmed and profited his associates. There was not a trace of hypocrisy about
him. He was absolutely true to the life he had
chosen.

Indeed, in austere living the new monk far exceeded his brethren. Soon so emaciated was he
by fasts and vigils that, as he glided through the
cloisters, a shadow rather than a man seemed to
have passed. He allowed himself but short intervals of sleep. Only after long and painful vigils did
his worn frame seek rest on a sack of straw and a

blanket. All his earthly goods were a few articles of clothing, and one or two religious books. Not because he preferred want and discomfort did Savonarola adopt this austere mode of life, but because it was the apparent spirit and practice of his order. He sought, also, by this complete withdrawal from worldly indulgence, to obtain closer communion with God. Simply as a means to this end was Savonarola an ascetic, "toiling to bring his heart and conscience into rest and peace with his divine Father."

The very opposite of an ascetic, Savonarola had a keen appreciation of the comforts of home, and of the beautiful in everything. He adorned his lectures and embellished his sermons with the lovely things of Scripture imagery. Any object that would set forth the beauty of the church as he loved to think of her, was eagerly employed— precious stones, white robes, crowns of life, palms of victory—anything. And he would have made home attractive by every adornment that was chaste and refining, everything that would win from the unclean world without.

Savonarola entered the convent expecting to find himself associated with only good and pure men. Could he have anticipated less? Had not the inmates—to a man—voluntarily renounced the world, and everything the human heart holds dear, in order to devote themselves to God? But did Girolamo find such companionship?—Far from it.

If the vice and pleasure-seeking of God-forgetting
Ferrara had so grieved him, how must he have felt
when he found the same iniquities flagrantly prac-
ticed beneath the hood and cowl? In vain did he
seek at Bologna one such man as his imagination
had pictured. Everyone gave evidence that he was
living far from God.

Amazed at these discoveries, Girolamo wept bitterly. It has been asserted that at no period since
the birth of Christ had the civilized world been in
so degraded a condition. History has recorded the
shameful lives of the Popes—Sixtus IV., Innocent
VIII., and Alexander VI., in whose reigns Savonarola lived. Their vices and crimes, together with
the miseries they entailed upon the people, constantly weighed down the spirit of the serious
young Dominican.

Added to this, he was sorely distressed over his
obligation to teach secular learning instead of the
divine word. With a heavy heart he performed
the task, endeavoring always, as he said, to "light
up his lectures with the simplicity of Christian faith,
and to avoid vain and useless questions."

When free to choose his subject for private study,
he turned eagerly to the word of God, and ever
found it the water of life to his thirsty spirit. Soon
after entering Bologna, Savonarola wrote the poem
" De Ruina Ecclesia"—"The Destruction of the
Church"—which strikingly indicates his line of
Scripture study during those early disappointing

days, it being replete with references to the Apoca-
lypse.  It is expressive also of burning indignation
against the monstrous corruptions of the church,
and breathes the most acute sorrow over the calam-
ities threatening Italy.

The special work assumed by the Dominican
order was "the preaching the gospel to the faithful scattered abroad."  And in 1478, three years
after his glad reception at Bologna, Savonarola was
elevated to the office of preacher, a post for which
his deep spirituality and his rare knowledge of the
Scriptures eminently qualified him.  Yet of his
sermons during the next four years nothing is
known, not even what impression they made upon
the brethren of his order.  About that time, however, one thus writes of him personally: " His voice
was harsh, his  gestures were awkward, and his
language ungraceful."

In January, 1482, after a residence of seven years
at Bologna, the Dominicans dispatched him on a
mission to the church in Ferrara.  One's natural
inference would be that now must his visits to the
paternal fireside have been frequent, and communion with his early friends have been revived.  Nothing could be farther from the truth.  He was
seldom seen in the abode of his parents, and in the
homes of his old associates, never.  Savonarola
vainly imagined that by thus crushing out the
affections God has implanted in the human heart,
he should the more successfully preach truth and

righteousness. In Ferrara his pulpit labors attracted little attention. This he lamented, remarking to his mother, "A prophet is always without honor in his own country." His sermons evinced high intellectual power, with great refinement of thought, and doubtless could not be appreciated by the frivolous Ferrarans.

That same year a fierce war broke out between Venice and Ferrara. The former, taking the lead. besieged the gay capital of Esté, dividing all Italy into two hostile parties, according as the provinces took side. The strife continued two years, when, by treaty, peace was restored. Ere the conflict really began, most of the Dominicans in Ferrara were ordered to leave their convent, Savonarola being sent to Florence, the city in which he reached the height of his brilliant career and which witnessed his martyrdom.

Bidding farewell to his parents and to Ferrara forever, he crossed the Apennines, and upon arrival in Florence, "went direct to the convent of San Marco."

Florence, the capital of Tuscany, lying on both banks of the Arno, was at that period one of the most corrupt cities in all Europe. The rich and powerful family of the Medici, fond of the arts, not less fond of display, and lavish in its contributions to the gay municipality, was the head of the government, and at the zenith of its popularity. Lorenzo de Medici, "The Magnificent," then in control at Florence, was the third generation from Giovanni de Medici, the founder of the house in 1426. His eldest son, Cosmo de Medici, was the grandfather of The Magnificent, Pietro I. being his father. The grandfather was the Astor of his age. He promoted commerce in Florence, and was a great patron of letters and philosophy. The grandson, Lorenzo, inherited his tastes and his ducats, and under his sway Florence enjoyed, outwardly, her golden days.

In its fine libraries and galleries of splendid paintings, the capital of Tuscany retains to-day something of its glory in the fifteenth century. The Uffizi Gallery contains masterpieces of those princes of art, Raphael and Titian. The Pitti collection embraced the finest works in the world. Its three large and valuable libraries are the resort of writers from almost every land on the globe. The Laurentian Library, attached to the convent of San Lorenzo, was once renowned as being the largest collection of books and manuscripts in Europe.

# CHAPTER IV.

## CONVENT OF SAN MARCO.

THE Convent of San Marco, situated near the gate San Gallo, in Florence, was long the most powerful monastery in Tuscany. A part of the extensive pleasure-grounds which surrounded the building in Savonarola's day, is now used as a botanical garden. Early in the fifteenth century the convent was almost in ruins, and was notable only for the infamous character of the monks who inhabited it, and who belonged to the order of San Sylvestro.

In 1436 one of the Medici—probably the elder Cosmo—obtained permission of the Pope to remove these monks and to place the structure in charge of the Dominicans of Lombardy. Thereupon the convent was immediately rebuilt, and as the years went by, was enriched and beautified by the Medici family. Within it Cosmo founded the first "public library opened in Italy," and in a short time the collection rivaled that of the far-famed library of San Lorenzo.

From all quarters of Italy now came scholars to consult its rare volumes, and to study the elegant paintings and frescoes which embellished the church and convent. The greatest works of Fra Giovanni di Fiesole were executed expressly for San Marco, where the heavenly-minded artist long wept and prayed. Of Fiesole's conceptions, radiant with angelic beauty, the great Michael Angelo once said: "He borrowed them from heaven to enrich and elevate the earth." His crowning work, "The Crucifixion," now adorns the ancient chapter house of San Marco.

Most of Fiesole's exquisite ideas were painted upon the *walls* of San Marco, while along its corridors and in its friars' cells was traced the sacred story of Christ's birth and death, by other hands as highly skilled. The "Announcement of the Saviour's Birth," by the brush of Cavallino, is considered wonderfully beautiful.

With Fiesole—well known as Fra Beato Angelico—painting was an act of religion, an expression of the faith, hope, and love which filled his heart. We are informed that it was his constant habit to ask the blessing of God upon his work before he began it, that it might be in some degree not unworthy of Him for whose glory it was attempted; and that whenever he felt an inward assurance that his prayer had been granted, he considered himself not at liberty to deviate in the slightest degree from the inspiration he had received.

Fiesole painted only sacred scenes, and "never for money." Any Florentine who desired a work from his brush had to apply to the prior of the con-

vent, and from him Angelico received the order.
Many a visitor to San Marco has been impressed
by the expression of sympathy in the faces of the
by-standers in Angelico's pictures of "The Crucifixion," "The Entombment," and "The Taking Down
from the Cross." But at this, one is not surprised,
when he learns that often when at work upon these
scenes, Fiesole wept as if present at them. It is the
artist's intense sympathy with Christ in his suffer-
ings, which gives those pieces their remarkable effect.

The equally eminent Bartolommeo, influenced by
Savonarola's lofty life, entered San Marco two years
after his death, and exerted his genius in adorning
the building wherein the martyr's final years had
been spent. In its refectory hangs a picture by the
famous Girlandajo. In the nave may be seen the
celebrated "Crucifix," from the brush of Giotto,
the first to give to the face of the dying Saviour an
expression of holy resignation, instead of a look of
mere physical agony.

These grand works of the old Italian masters
have always drawn lovers of art to San Marco, and
more especially since within its cloisters linger
precious memories of the great Dominican monk.
His cell, of two chambers, and larger than most of
the others, remains nearly in the same condition as
on the day he went forth from it to torture and to
death. There were many who loved the gifted
man, and found comfort in preserving his chair, the

couch so often wet with his tears, the robes he laid aside, and his portrait, taken years before, when to paint Savonarola was almost the highest opportunity an artist could enjoy.

Shortly after his martyrdom, the following inscription was placed over his cell as an evidence of the love his convent bore him: "That apostolic man, Francesco Jerome Savonarola, occupied these cells." How this inscription escaped the destructive hand of his enemies—the Medici—is a mystery. It has been suggested as a reason that the man's republicanism, demanding the utmost sacrifice of his worldly interests, was altogether too unattractive to induce many to espouse its principles. Hence such reminders of him could do little harm.

Savonarola delighted in true art as thoroughly as did the Medici, and at San Marco his refined tastes were fully gratified by the paintings and sculptures within the convent, by the lovely flowers blooming about him as he walked around its grounds, or by the charming scenes which opened to his view. Taking seat in some secluded spot, he would take his psalter from his pocket, and turn its pages until he found a text for every scene and object. Thus everything declared to him the glory and love of God. He was delighted. He feasted upon the truth, upon the exquisite things at every turn, and hoped that at San Marco he should find the purity and the peace for which he longed at Bologna.

But did he? Could he, as he came to know them,
3

trace in one of his brethren the image of the self-
denying Christ? For his sake they professed to
have renounced the world. Were they striving
to be like him?—Not one of them. His name was
seldom, if ever, on their lips. In not one of them
reigned his spirit. Pained to the depths of his soul,
Savonarola once more shrank from association with
brethren false and hasting into every evil path.

"A feeling of scorn, almost of disgust, for secular study arose within him." He would ask himself: To what good, to what right purpose, has it
ever tended? Of what value is Aristotle, this pros-
tration to paganism, which renders the cross of
Christ distasteful? With such thoughts and feelings he found not one to sympathize. He could
induce not one to study the Scriptures with him.
So entirely was the word of God, particularly
the Old Testament, neglected, that a monk much
respected in San Marco, once gravely asked:
"What possible good can be derived from the
knowledge of events so long since accomplished?"
But this ignorance in a mere monk need not surprise us, for long after, Rome, through Pope Leo
X., boasted that "the fable of Jesus Christ had
served the church in good stead."

In Lent, 1483, Savonarola preached his first sermon in Florence. The attempt was an utter failure,
so his audience deemed. The sermon was given in
the church of San Lorenzo. Great things had been
expected of the new preacher. His learning and

piety had been widely heralded. His graceful figure and expressive face promised to attract. But
how harsh and repelling were his tones! how uncultivated his gestures! how dry and scholastic his
style! At his third sermon scarcely five and twenty
persons occupied the vast nave of the church.

During the same Lent, there was preaching at
Florence, in the church of Santo Spirito, a great
favorite of the Medici—Marriano Gennezzano—a
speaker of "sonorous voice, choice sentences, and
noble language." To him now flocked the crowds,
and San Lorenzo was deserted. Yet at the present
day, while public interest in Savonarola is greatly increasing, Gennezzano is remembered only as a man
who, a few years later, did his utmost at Rome, to
accomplish the downfall and death of the great
Dominican.

"Elegance of language must give way to simplicity in preaching the truth," averred Savonarola.
Yet most keenly did he feel his unpopularity. It
was a trial which would have crushed him utterly
but for his profound consecration. Sometimes the
thought entered his mind that he had better con-
fine himself to teaching the novices in San Marco,
but the very next moment it was rejected. "Preach
against the widespread iniquity of the church he
must. Silent he could not be." He would overcome his defects. If not, he would rise above them.

Deeply reflecting over all these things, he earnestly prayed that God would use him as an instru-

ment for purifying the church, and sometimes exclaimed: "Are not the Florentines, like the Heb-
rews of old, ungrateful, rebellious? Shall I not call
them to repentance?" But the lively Florentines
turned deaf ears.

About this time Savonarola developed a new
phase of character, or of faith. He had come to
believe that disclosures of future events were made
to him by the Lord. One day, while conversing
with one of the friars, there appeared to him a scene
in which the heavens parted before him, and gazing
into their depths, he read the dire declaration that
wrath had been decreed by the Lord against Italy
and the church, and as he stood awestruck, a voice
in the distance bade him declare to the people the
vision he had seen. Profoundly impressed, he exclaimed: "Oh, that my voice could reach to the
ends of the earth!"

During this year, 1483, occurred the death of
the corrupt Pope, Sixtus IV. His successor was
Innocent VIII., whose election well-nigh produced
schism in the church. In morality, he was no im-
provement upon his predecessor. Soon, at his
court every class of iniquity flourished. A writer
of that day, contrasting the ghastly vice of Italy
with the purer life of Northern Europe, affirms:
"The nearer a people lives to the court of Rome,
the less religion it has. Were that court set down
among the Swiss, who still remain pious, they too
would soon be corrupted." Upon reading these

words, Guicciardini remarked: "Whatever evil may be said of the Roman court must fall short of the truth."

As the days grew darker in the experience of the church, Savonarola mourned, fasted, and prayed the more devoutly. Prostrate before the Lord, he bathed the altar steps with tears. Most opportunely for him, he was now sent to San Geminiano—a mountain village not far away—to preach the Lent sermons of 1484. More at ease among the simple peasantry, Savonarola candidly said: " I declare it upon the authority of Scripture. The church will be scourged, then regenerated, and speedily." This was his first utterance of the kind; but later, in the Duomo at Florence, they were often reiterated, not simply upon the "authority of Scripture," but *as a direct revelation from God* to himself.

A missionary occasion called the earnest monk to Lombardy in 1486. Here, at Brescia, he preached the Lent sermons. Now every vestige of infirmity in utterance had vanished. With a voice of thunder he aroused the souls of men. Thousands were soon upon their knees in the church. Moved by his vehement words, they pressed toward the pulpit. Then, " leaning over the desk, he spoke to them words which made them weep and tremble, and ever after lived in their memory."

As on many former occasions, his text was from the Revelation. Oppressed by the frightful condition of Italy, by the sins of both clergy and

people, he could preach of nothing but approaching judgment.  In tremulous tones he foretold that
ere long Brescia would be attacked, that blood
would flow through its streets, that parents would
be seen weeping for their children and for each
other.  He assured them that some then living
would witness these scenes, and perhaps even those
listening to his warning.  Himself awed by his
words, Savonarola paused, raised himself in the pulpit, looked around upon the stricken people, and
called upon them to repent ; to turn every one to
the Lord, who would abundantly have mercy.

To the people, from that hour, Savonarola was a
prophet of God.  He knew it; and by prayers and
fastings more frequent, strove to be worthy of the
high vocation to which he truly believed God had
called him.

After that day, twenty-six years, Brescia was involved in war.  Six thousand of its citizens lay
dead in its streets, slain by the merciless troops of
Gaston de Foix.  Of the surviving inhabitants some
there were who recalled the prediction uttered by
that impassioned monk, Girolamo Savonarola, in
1486, and who twelve years after "had joined the
great army of martyrs."

Four years Savonarola passed in Lombardy,—
years of steady preparation for the following few
years of work and victory.  In January, 1490, he
preached at Genoa during Lent, and thence returned to Florence.  On the journey to Genoa he

wrote his mother a letter filled with expressions of
tender love. We condense it, unwillingly, for our
pages.

"HONORED MOTHER : The peace of Christ be with
you. You must be surprised that I have not
written you for many days. It has not been for
want of thought for you, but for lack of a messenger. I met with no one going from Brescia to
Ferrara until one of our own people arrived here
after the Feast of the Nativity, with whom I was so
much engaged that, to my great regret, I quite forgot to write. I can well imagine that you have
been in much tribulation, and so far as my frailty
will allow, I pray to God continually for you. I
know not what more I can do. Could I help you in
any other way, I would'do so. >I have voluntarily
given myself to be a slave for the love of Jesus, who,
for love of me, took the part of a slave to set me
free. I am bound to use the talent he has given
me, in the way most pleasing to him. I fear his
condemnation were I to do otherwise.

"Be not, therefore, displeased, my most dear
mother, if I go far from you, and if I go about
preaching in various cities. I do it for the salvation
of souls, and not for any other object. Moreover,
I am sent by my superiors to perform that work.
You ought, therefore, to take comfort, that God has
elected one of your offspring to so high an office.
It is a calling for which I cannot be too grateful.
Therefore, my most honored mother, grieve not on
my account.

"I thought to send but a few lines, but my love has made my pen run on, and more than I had thought of doing I have laid open my heart to you. Know then, finally, that more than ever, my heart is fixed to devote soul and body, and all the knowledge God has given me, for the salvation of my neighbors; and as I cannot do it in my own country, I do it elsewhere.

"This day, as soon as I have dined, I proceed to Genoa. Pray to God that he may lead me thither in safety, and enable me to bring forth fruit among the people. Remember me to my uncle, aunt, and cousins. May the grace of God be with you, and keep you from all harm, for the love of our Lord Jesus Christ, Amen.

"Written in Pavia on the day of the conversion of St. Paul, the apostle. Your son,

"FRATE HIERONYMO SAVONAROLA."

# CHAPTER V.

## UNEXPECTED FAME.

BY invitation of Lorenzo, The Magnificent, Savonarola returned from Lombardy to Florence in 1491. His recall was at the entreaty of Prince Pico della Mirandola, famous for his learning at the early age of twenty-three, and one of the most noble men of that age. The two young men had met not long before at a Dominican counsel held at Reggio. Fascinated with Savonarola, from that hour until the day of his own early death, he remained the unswerving friend of the fearless and peerless preacher. We are constrained not to proceed with this narrative until we have pictured to our readers Savonarola as he appeared in that council at Reggio.

Owing much to wearing fasts and vigils, his bodily presence was at first sight little calculated to attract attention. As he sits apart from his brethren, he is but a grave and gentle-looking monk. See, his frame is fragile. His hands are so emaciated that, held before the light, they are quite transparent. Yet the face, with cowled head rising above the black mantle and the white tunic, is striking. The eyes of unearthly brightness, and

(41)

shaded by long lashes, are soft but penetrating. Now he rises to speak. All eyes are drawn to him. In every gesture, every movement, beams forth the spirit in the man. His countenance becomes radiant. His eyes dart flashes of lightning. His eloquence is like a torrent. His intellectual power is princely. His warnings are like thunder-bolts. "From that day the soul of Pico was knit to that of the speaker, in bonds which death alone could sever." Is it any wonder then that we find the gifted prince urging Lorenzo de Medici to invite the wonderful monk to Florence?

Ripened in thought and purpose, Savonarola resumed his lectures in lovely San Marco. To his surprise he was famous. Prince Pico had heralded his coming. That was sufficient. Learned Florentines begged permission to attend his lectures. In the cloister garden, among the damask roses, the once rejected monk now explained to them his choicest book—the Revelation. His audience increased day by day. Soon the garden could not hold the half who came to hear. They then besought him to lecture from the chapel pulpit. He replied, "Pray to the Lord for me." A few days later he stated to the people: "To-morrow I will speak in the church. There will be a lecture and a sermon."

On that "to-morrow" the church was crowded. It was August 1, 1491. With the crucifix in one hand and the Bible in the other, Savonarola entered the pulpit. Deeming himself called as by a voice from heaven, he preached with the authority of a prophet of the Lord, and proclaimed an impending crisis in the church. Everything, he affirmed, "tends to that end—the measure of iniquity, full to overflowing, the appalling moral condition, the neglected doctrines of truth, displaced, even in the minds of the clergy, by fables of astrology and soothsaying."

The excitement caused by this sermon was intense. And yet Savonarola was not elated. The next discourse might be uttered only to empty benches. Of all places Florence was most fickle and ungrateful. Remembering this, and wishing to perpetuate any good his sermons might contain, he resolved to publish them. Previous to that date few had been preserved; but of those preached between that time and his death, a large number remain. Savonarola himself called this first sermon preached in the church of the convent, "a terrible discourse," and while delivering it, he predicted, so we find, that he should preach eight years. He did; and then followed torture and martyrdom.

His hearers multiplied by thousands, and soon the great speaker deserted the convent chapel for the ampler audience room of the Duomo—the church of "Santa Maria del Fiore." There he again declared in tones of absolute assurance: "The day of vengeance is at hand. The chastisement will be inflicted, that Italy and the church, purified in

the furnace, may rise to a holy and happy state."
The people, fascinated, awe-struck, eagerly listened.
Then, choosing the right moment, and lowering his
voice, he spoke tenderly of mercy exercised in the
midst of judgment. Pausing now, he kissed the
crucifix, pressed it to his heart, and in accents most
gentle and loving, directed them to Him who died
that penitent sinners might live.

"For seven years from that day, Savonarola was
master both of the pulpit and people in Florence."

His popularity alarmed Lorenzo. Five eminent
Florentines were sent to him to recommend language less exciting. "I am fully aware," said Savonarola, "that you have been sent to me by
Lorenzo. Return to him, and tell him from me to
repent of his sins, for the Lord spares no one, and
fears not the princes of this world." "Take care,"
rejoined one of the messengers, "that your bold
words do not bring you into exile." "Do you
threaten me with banishment?" returned Savonarola. "Go, tell Lorenzo that though I am a stranger
and he the first man in Florence, it is I that shall
remain, and he shall depart." That startling utterance was prophetic, as we shall soon see.

One year had Savonarola been in Florence when
he was made prior of San Marco by Lorenzo de
Medici. It was customary for him who received
this appointment to pay his respects to its giver.
The new prior refused to concede to the custom,
saying: "I regard God as the author of my elec-

tion. Let us, therefore, go into the chapel and return thanks to him." Lorenzo was highly incensed. He broke out:—

"See, now, here is a stranger come into my house, who refuses to visit me!" And yet open hostility was not the fruit of the prior's independence. Lorenzo preferred to win him by other means. He sent an official to enrich the alms-box, and himself took walks in the beautiful convent grounds, hoping incidentally to meet the dauntless man. Savonarola perceived his intent and remained in his cloister. Little did the Medici then imagine that he had invited to Florence, in the person of this preacher, one who would prove a relentless enemy to the house of Medici. He could not but respect the man. He was too strong to resist. So, himself breaking in health, he left Savonarola to pursue his high mission, and all the more as he perceived that the Florentines, mightily influenced by the prior, were drawn from the senseless amusements he had provided, to the services of religion.

# CHAPTER VI.

## THE DEATH OF LORENZO.

THE year 1492 saw the most illustrious of the Medici pass away. At Careggi, three miles from Florence, Lorenzo owned a delightful villa. Here, in April, ill in bed, he realized that he was about to die. Little thought had the great patron of art ever given to preparation for eternity. None of his treasures were laid up in heaven. But they enriched the libraries and art galleries of Florence. Of the lofty spirituality of the Christian religion he had no conception. He believed in future retribution for the wicked. Facing that future now, he trembled exceedingly.

Many a time had he done what the word of God forbids—oppressed the widow, the fatherless, and the poor. Like specters, now stood all these deeds before him. The Catholic Church had indeed taught him that all the evil he had done was amply "justified by the necessities of his position." But in this trying hour conscience did not seem to agree with the church. He therefore desired the guidance of someone who would not swerve from the truth. He knew of but one such man in the church.

(46)

That man was the independent prior of St. Mark's. For Savonarola, therefore, he sent, saying to the messenger : " Make haste. Delay not."

Did the prior now refuse to call upon the prince, as when he had received from his hand the appointment to San Marco?—No, truly. Assured that Lorenzo lay at the door of death, and that he desired to see him, Savonarola started instantly for Careggi. Arrived at the villa, he found sitting at the bedside of the duke the noble Prince Pico, the loyal friend of both men. The prince at once withdrew, leaving the dying Medici and the priest together. Turning to Savonarola, Lorenzo said there were three things which oppressed his conscience, and for which he desired to be forgiven. These were: The cruel destruction of Volterra, the appropriating to himself monies intended as marriage portions for the daughters of its citizens, and the shedding of innocent blood in Florence after the Pazzi conspiracy.

Savonarola immediately spoke to him of the tender compassion and mercy of that God whom he had offended, and then added: " But, three things are necessary before you can hope for the pardon of your sins." " What things, father ? " asked Lorenzo, steadily searching the friar's face. " In the first place, it is necessary that you have a strong and lively faith in God." Lorenzo answered : "That I have, most fully." " In the second place, it is absolutely essential that you restore, or leave directions to have restored, all that you unjustly took away."

That was a terrible demand. Lorenzo hesitated a moment, and then assented by a movement of the head. " Lastly," continued the priest, " you must restore liberty to the commonwealth of Florence." How severe was this condition Savonarola fully realized, and with intense anxiety awaited the answer. None ever came. "Lorenzo turned his face to the wall and remained silent." Savonarola returned to San Marco leaving the prince unabsolved. April 8 witnessed his death.

Florence greatly lamented him. Why?—He had most abundantly enriched her; most liberally amused her. All Italy regarded his death as an irreparable loss. Why?—Because learned men, lovers of art in every province, had felt the magic influence of his liberality. Not long before the death of The Magnificent, Savonarola had predicted it, in the presence of three distinguished Florentines, together with that of Ferdinand, king of Naples, and of Pope Innocent VIII. Lorenzo and the Pope had already passed away, and January 23, 1494, King Ferdinand also fell asleep.

The death of the Medici and of the Pope, so soon following the prediction,—Innocent died July 26, 1492,—joined to the fact that before his death Lorenzo had sent for the friar, and also to the marvelous circumstance that the latter had refused the prince absolution, were occurrences which mightily

increased the popularity of Savonarola, and unfortunately opened the way for him to act his part in
the political scenes about to take place.

Lorenzo was succeeded by his son Pietro de
Medici, whose distinguished incapacity for government rendered him unpopular from the first. And
very soon there was formed a party opposed to him,
and chiefly of men who in the days of Lorenzo
were steadfast friends of the Medici.

Let us now glance at Italian affairs outside of
Florence. Through certain political combinations,
which we need not mention in detail, and above all,
through the extremely corrupt character of Pope
Alexander VI., successor of Innocent VIII., matters
began to grow very dark all over Italy. As the
gloom deepened, many recalled to mind that just
such a time of woe had been foretold by "that
saintly preacher, the prior of San Marco." This
wonderfully added to Savonarola's fame. The sul-
len events themselves had the effect to rivet in the
depths of his soul the conviction that the gift of
prophecy had been vouchsafed to him. More and
more then did the pages of the Old Testament
prophets furnish him food for thought.

While preaching an advent sermon, during that
lowering time, he beheld the heavens part asunder,
and, as if suspended in the air, a hand grasping a
drawn sword, upon which was inscribed, "The
sword of the Lord upon the earth, and speedily."
As he gazed, dumb with awe, gentle words fell on

4

his ear, "Mercy would be mingled with judgment for all the penitent." Then, in sterner tones, the voice threatened " sure and terrible doom for all the hardened." Then suddenly the sword was turned toward the earth; the air grew dark; there fell showers of swords and arrows mingled with fire; famine desolated the earth, and fearful thunders shook the ground. The vision then vanished, and a voice charged the monk to tell the people what he had seen and heard, that they might repent, and in the day of the Lord's vengeance find shelter.

The year following the death of Lorenzo, Savon- arola preached the Lent sermons at Bologna, at- tended by one Fra Basilio, whom he styles his much- loved son. Among the crowds who came to hear was the wife of the Lord of Bologna. Always late and attended by a retinue of ladies and gentlemen, she much disturbed the services. On several occa- sions Savonarola quietly paused until they were seated. But finally, becoming weary of the inter- ruptions, he one day said, "My lady, you would please God and give me great satisfaction by com- ing earlier hereafter." Her ladyship's next attend- ance was with still greater pomp and noise. Then, as she proceeded to her accustomed seat, the preacher, forgetting for a moment the value of self- control, said, " It is the devil come to interrupt the worship of God."

Infuriated, the woman ordered two of her attend- ants to seize him on the spot. Prudence forbade such a step, and no one moved. Determined, however,

to take his life, she that evening dispatched two men
to the convent where he tarried, to assassinate him.
The porter, suspecting their errand, declined to
admit them, and informed Savonarola of their presence and of his own fears. "Admit them," replied
he; "my trust is in God."

Having entered, the men stood mutely gazing at
him. "What is your business?" calmly asked the
friar. Overcome by his serene manner, they inaptly
faltered out: "Our lady sends us to say that she is
ready to supply you with anything you may re-
quire!" "Return my thanks to your lady," said
Savonarola, and the men retired. They could not
touch him. His hour had not yet come.

At the close of his last sermon in Bologna Savonarola announced: "I shall this evening leave
Bologna with my walking stick"—Savonarola made
all his journeys on foot—"and wooden flask. If
anyone has anything to say to me, let him come to
me before I leave. My death will not be celebrated
at Bologna." Even that early, he seemed to have
an inward conviction that his death would not occur
out of Florence. That evening, accompanied by
his friend, Fra Basilio, he set out on the journey
over the Apennines.

The uneasiness of the Florentines under the sway
of Pietro de Medici, with the Prince's too apparent
enmity toward himself, sorely burdened the weary
prior as he drew near the city. As he pursued his
way, faint and foot-sore, there appeared to him
suddenly a supernatural personage—evidently to

strengthen the sinking wayfarer—who attended him to the gate San Gallo and then disappeared, after uttering this note of warning, " Remember that thou doest that for which thou art sent by God."

This incident is related by Savonarola's biographer, Burlamacchi, one of his constant and appreciative hearers. Viewed in the light of the period in which Savonarola lived, and of the church in which he was nurtured, it does not impress one as at all remarkable. And, indeed, regarded even from a Protestant standpoint, the circumstance is credible. No one can affirm but that in all ages God's consecrated servants, in moments of despondency, or of physical weakness, or in hours of great peril, have been sustained by heavenly messengers, sent to cheer, strengthen, or help. It is the word of God which asks with reference to angels: "Are they not all ministering spirits, sent forth to minister for them who shall be heirs of salvation?" Notice: It is only to those who shall be heirs of salvation that they minister.

We give prominence to these oft-repeated visions, because, as we think, they prodigiously influenced his choice of the unwise course which terminated in his shameful martyrdom. If any other influence was greater, it was that produced by his wrapt and constant study of the Old Testament prophecies, and of the Revelation. Certainly these two forces did very much toward giving the man's life the contour it presents to us at the distance of four centuries from his time.

# CHAPTER VII.

THAT Savonarola was an intensely practical worker, as well as a man influenced by supernatural sights, was clearly apparent upon his return to San Marco. For some time discipline in the convent had been so relaxed, and the moral and spiritual tone within it so depressed, as to imperil its little society. This state of things he now determined to improve. Up to this time San Marco had been ruled by the Dominican vicars of Lombardy. Savonarola secured a papal order releasing the convent from their control. Thus he became supreme in authority, subject only to the Pope, and could accomplish his reforms.

So uncongenial previously had been the life at San Marco that he had thought seriously of withdrawing from it; but now, as he believed, he was in the place divinely appointed for him, and he would there do his duty. He himself tells us his desire was "not to make mere hermits of his brethren, but good religious men, who should lead holy lives, and for the salvation of men be ready to shed their blood." He looked into the future with the brightest hope. He and his consecrated friars should rekindle faith, arouse a sleeping world.

(53)

Enormous possessions had been brought into the convent.  His first step was to revive the vow of poverty.  Had not the last words of St. Dominic, who founded the order, been, "Be charitable, preserve humility, practice poverty with cheerfulness," followed by the awful malediction : " May my curse and that of God fall upon him who shall bring possessions into this order."  No longer should these words remain a dead letter.  Upon the walls of San Marco should they now be inscribed.  " Men shall hear them again," declared Savonarola, as he paced the cloisters absorbed in thought, or gazed upon Fra Angelico's portrait of St. Dominic, until he almost heard that curse fall from his lips. "Again and again had the vow of poverty been broken.  And the other vows, had they been kept? Times without number had they been infringed."

In order to sustain the convent without gifts, Savonarola devised courses of instruction in sculp-- ture, painting, architecture, illuminating and copying of manuscripts.  Lay brethren and friars who were not qualified to teach, or to study in the classes, were furnished some suitable employment, and thus soon all were at work.  Greek, Hebrew, and other languages which would aid in the study of Scripture, were also taught in San Marco.

Throughout this entire system of renewing, Savonarola was the living illustration of the principles he advocated.  In study, in self-denial, in obedience to discipline, he led them all.  If strict with the members, he was more so with himself.  His raiment was coarser, his bed harder, his cell more scantily furnished than theirs.  Thus was the entire tone of life in the convent elevated, and the institution grew rapidly in reputation.

Admission within its walls was sought, as a high

favor, by the first citizens of Florence. And neighboring convents desired to join the Tuscan Congregation, that they might be allied to San Marco. With reference to the latter petitions, Savonarola moved cautiously, always referring them to the Pope. But gladly would he have welcomed all the *Dominicans* of Tuscany around San Marco. In reference to this, however, humiliation was in store for him. Of the forty-four friars in Pisa, only four would consent to the union. At Siena, while making a tour to accomplish this object, the authorities drove him from the city. He withdrew and returned to Florence, meeting with a cordial welcome.

It was during Lent of this year, probably 1495, that Savonarola preached a series of sermons that specially set forth the doctrines he wished to stamp indelibly upon the minds of the people. They were the very doctrines enforced a quarter of a century later by Luther, Zwingle, Knox, and Calvin. Yet they were proclaimed and eagerly accepted early in the reign of Alexander VI., the worst of popes, and in Italy the very stronghold of the Papacy, by great numbers who listened to Savonarola at San Marco and elsewhere.

In this year, too, occurred the remarkable coincidence of Savonarola preaching " faith in Christ as the gift of God, for the salvation of every believer," and the revival of " that accursed tribunal," the Spanish Inquisition. Midnight times they were, " when priests governed politically and princes ruled ecclesiastically." Church and State were one. The Pope was both a temporal prince and the " Head of the Church." But the dawn of a better day was at hand. Savonarola was in the full tide of his career, fearlessly denouncing " priestly princes and princely priests," neither fearing nor favoring man. And God greatly honored him; used him to blaze the trees for the grand reformers soon to follow him.

No class of men were so severely rebuked as the clergy. "Why," he would ask, "do they tickle ears with Aristotle, Virgil, Plato, Plutarch? Why do they not instead, teach that in which is the law and the spirit of life?" Often he said: "The gospel, my brethren, must be your constant companion. I speak not of the *book* but of its *spirit*. Having not the spirit of grace, it will avail nothing, though you carry about the whole volume."

It is beyond denial that Savonarola's appreciation of Scripture was very far in advance of his time. It was said there is not a text to which he could not turn in a moment. A vast portion of the Bible he knew by heart. Better still, by constant prayer and study, its words had become to him the voice of its divine Author, revealing unto him the mightiest truths. Savonarola's devout love of the life-giving word begat in him a burning desire that laity and clergy should study it. He wanted every home in Italy, every class of people, to be blessed by it.

He would sometimes exclaim: "People of Florence, give yourselves to the study of God's word! The highest blessing is to understand it. Let us publicly confess the fact that the Scriptures have been locked up. Their light has been almost extinguished, been set aside, left in the dust."

This was a caustic and brave charge to make against the Catholic Church. For who but she had extinguished the light of the Scriptures. Had she not hung, burned, tortured, imprisoned, by every mode punished and put to death, thousands of God's children for no other crime than that of secretly reading and teaching his word?

Savonarola Preaching.

We next hear him demolish that fatal system of
Mary-worship, which is but an invention of the
same power.  Listen to him : " You may, perhaps,
inquire why I so rarely preach about the virgin,
since she is in highest degree to be praised.  And
I beg to ask you why the Holy Spirit has in so few
instances made mention of her in the Scriptures ?
and why the primitive saints preached so little about
her?  Should you reply, 'The people are now more
devoted to her than were the early fathers and
saints,' I should deem such an answer nothing to
the purpose, nor even credible; for the apostles,
who so much loved and honored her,have made
little or no mention of her.  How did this happen?
The apostles have not written of her because *our
salvation depends on faith in Christ*, and they, being
wholly bent on this fact, *preached nothing but Christ.*
In consequence of the great light they had from
God, their views were wholly fixed on him, not
on the creature.

" Besides, had the apostles recorded the praises of
the virgin, dwelt on her profound humility, her immense charity, and her other boundless virtues, the
people *would probably have read the gospel of the
virgin* more than *the gospel of the acts of Christ*,
and would have *made a divinity of her.*  Since, then,
the object of the apostles was to exalt Christ, and
to prove that he alone is God, he alone is the Mes-
siah who came to save the world, I, like them,
have attempted to preach according to the Scripture; and since the Scripture makes little mention
of the virgin, my habit has been not to speak much
of her."

Listen, also, to his ringing words on faith.  They
render San Marco's eloquent prior not unworthy a
place among those who felled the trees and bridged

the streams before the noble army yet to come, on whose banners should be inscribed, "The just shall live by faith." "In faith everything depends on appropriation. Not only must we say, 'Thou art king, O God,' but, 'Thou art my king and my God, my God whom I desire. My God in whom I trust.' Every confidence in ourselves is false. That confidence, alone, which is based on Jesus Christ is just. His merit is boundless and of boundless power. Its source is in the Godhead. It comes from the might which is in Jesus without measure." These words were a torch uplifted amid great darkness. He uttered many more like them.

They place Savonarola—with Tauler in Germany, Huss in Bohemia, Wycliffe in England—among the grand heralds of the reformation, which, led by Luther, was to burst forth in the next century. Indeed, his connection with that movement was much closer than is generally supposed.

It was in Florence, during the years of his highest usefulness at San Marco, that by his glowing words he aroused a fervent love of the truth in such earnest young English scholars as John Linacre, for a time tutor to the children of Lorenzo de Medici; as John Colet, afterward Dean of St. Paul's in London and Biblical lecturer at Oxford; as William Grocyn, divinity professor at Exeter College; as William Lilly, the first teacher of Greek in the city of London.

Drawn by enthusiasm for the learning which Lorenzo delighted to foster, these and other Oxford students went to Florence to study. They returned to England bringing not only a revival of art and literature from the court of Lorenzo, but also a revival of deep spirituality from the cloisters of San Marco. What they had learned and experienced

soon took firm hold in the churches, lecture-rooms,
and college halls of England.  Noted among these
young men became John Colet.   In fact, no better
fruit of his labors did Savonarola leave behind him
than the conversion of this heroic Englishman.

We may profitably take space to here summarize
the life of Colet.   He was a son of the Lord Mayor
of London, a son, too, of fortune, but destined to a
life of constant well-doing.   Almost with the eyes
of the great Italian preacher he seemed to see the
corruption existing in high places.   He declared:
"Unless there can be a reform of the clergy, from
the Pope down, through all grades, I see no chance
of saving the church.   O Jesus Christ," he cried,
"wash for us not our feet only, but also our hands
and our *head!*   Otherwise our disordered church
cannot be far from death."

John Colet, subjected to the most violent asper-
sions, waged a fierce battle against the destructive
"methods and principles of the schoolmen.   From
their dogmatism he revolted with all his soul."
His study of Greek in Florence had opened to him
the New Testament, the vivifying facts of the gospel
story, the edifying letters of the apostles.   And
soon he began to teach the truths he had learned.
For his pay he was charged with "making infidels"!

John Colet was the first link, next to Savonarola.
Now mark the next link.   John Colet could teach
Greek.   In Holland lived a young student, eager
for the "new learning," but too poor to go into
Italy, to the schools of the Medici.   He worked his
passage to England, and came to John Colet to be
taught Greek.   This was the to-be-famous Erasmus
of Rotterdam.   Colet taught him something besides Greek.   Soon the pupil excelled the master.
Erelong the keenest pen of that age was holding up

to the contempt they deserved, monkish ignorance and priestly pretension.

This is not all. Erasmus gave an immense influence to the Reformation, by editing the Greek Testament with a Latin translation. "The book became the talk of the universities." Reading it, men were for the first time brought into vivifying contact with the life of Christ. That book fell into the hands of Thomas Bilney, a poor student like Erasmus, endeavoring by fastings and vigils to obtain ease for a troubled conscience; a man buying masses and indulgences; a man wondering if anywhere a guide could be found. Erasmus is the second link from Savonarola, Thomas Bilney is the third.

As he opened the Testament, these words fell under his eye. "This is a faithful saying, and worthy of all acceptation, that Christ Jesus came into the world to save sinners." He afterward said: "This one sentence, through the power of God working on my soul, rejoiced my heart, deeply wounded by a sense of sin, and almost in the depths of despair, I felt an inward comfort which I cannot describe. My broken heart rejoiced."

While Bilney was at Cambridge, there was passing through the divinity school a hot young papist, with heart full of hatred against the new opinions, and against those who denounced the vices of the priesthood. So zealous was his ecclesiasticism that the university made him its official cross-bearer, that is, the bearer of the great silver cross in the university parades and processions. Upon taking his degree as bachelor of divinity, this young Catholic made a spiteful attack against the gentle Philip Melancthon.

Thomas Bilney heard the oration, and discovered

in it tokens that, mentally, its author was ill at ease; that he needed to know just what he, Thomas Bilney, had experienced. He followed him to his study and entreated him to hear him. As both were in the same church fold, the young divine listened. Bilney told him the pitiable story of his own struggle, how he had "done penance, had paid for masses and absolutions, had fasted, wept, prayed, until almost in despair." In short, he had used all the remedies the young man's oration had recommended. At last he read the book forbidden to the people by the church, and therein found the knowledge of God's free gift in Jesus Christ, and so found peace. "And now," asked Bilney, "must I go back to penance and despair?"

"Bilney's frank and simple story," said the young priest afterwards, "revealed to me more of myself than I ever before knew." Long had he craved the peace and health of mind Bilney now possessed. With all his soul he sought it and found it. He was one of the university preachers. Soon he began to preach mightily the doctrine of eternal life as a *free gift*, through Jesus Christ, to every penitent soul. He was a man called to preach before kings. He was a man to suffer martyrdom by burning. He was Hugh Latimer, Bishop of Worcester, peer of the realm, and the fourth link from Savonarola. We are now in the full tide of the Reformation.

# CHAPTER VIII.

E have seen that the "revival of learning" —as it was termed—in Italy, under the sway of the Medici, including the study of Greek especially, led to large increase of spiritual life in England. In Italy the result was different. There the tendency was strong toward everything ancient, whether in art or in books. And this was simply a running after paganism. Whatever was heathenish in painting, in sculpture, in pottery, in books, was welcomed, admired, treasured. More than all his cotemporaries, Lorenzo de Medici fostered this taste. The furor swept into the church. Scarcely a vestige or semblance of Christianity remained in it. Essentially the people were heathen amid all the splendor. "Italy was the darkest spot in all Christendom," remarks one in speaking of that period. This inclination backward and downward Savonarola clearly saw from the moment he entered Florence. The state of things sorely troubled him. Everywhere he protested against it. As soon as possible he meant to effect a reform, in every line of literature especially. No sooner was he prior of San Marco than he began the work. Did his condemnation include all ancient literature?— Far from it. Few men were better versed in the classics than Savonarola. But the enthusiastic study of pagan authors and pagan art had corrupted the Christian faith, and displaced the Holy Script-

{63}

ures. These, and not Greek fables, he believed to be the basis of all true education. Why should Livy and Thucydides engross the whole attention of students, and the historians of the Old Testament be neglected? he would ask.

The study of the Old Testament was his delight, as has already been remarked. And when he would lead others into its rich fields, his words were spoken with thrilling effect. Often the telling of what he himself had found therein changed the plan and purpose of a human life. To too great an extent, perhaps, he attached a spiritual meaning to everything. But this faculty gave him an immense influence in teaching and preaching, as well as in quiet, earnest talks with friends. Thus, in urging the Florentines to shun intellectual idolatry, his prohibitions were strengthened and supported by text after text of Scripture. From every wandering path he brought them straight back to its lessons.

"Isaac," he said, "commanded not to take a wife of the daughters of Canaan, warned Christians not to seek truth in heathen writings." "The Jews, loathing manna in the wilderness, and sighing for the flesh-pots of Egypt, prefigured those who have the word of God but neglect it for the study of pagan philosophy." To this symbolism he added the noble exhortation to "believe in the all-sufficiency of the word, and in the wisdom of Christ, who has left his precepts so clearly expressed *that no human wisdom is required to explain them.*" How contradictory is this last statement to the teaching of the papal church, which maintains that the common people *cannot* understand the Scriptures, and should not read them without explanation by the priests.

He exclaimed: "Go into all the schools of Florence, and you will find professors paid to teach logic and philosophy, the arts and sciences, but not one paid to undertake the teaching of Holy Scripture. Dost thou not perceive that faith is degraded by resting it on the profane sciences? Call to mind David going forth to meet Goliath, and, laying aside the armor of pagan study, arm thyself with a lively and simple faith, after the example of the apostles and martyrs."

Prodigious was the evil effect of this exclusive cultivation of classical literature. All branches of education suffered from it. The standard of excellence in art was found in pagan models. Not only so, artists often selected their models from the most unworthy classes. "Madonnas, Magdalens, and saints were picked up anywhere, and under the artist's transforming hand became holy, humble men and women, and even glorified saints." Before such pictures the people paid homage. To Savonarola the thought of all this was torture. At the same time he realized that the mere putting away of impure things would not secure purity of heart. So, with all the energy of his soul, he implored his people to strive after inward cleanliness.

As he no doubt anticipated, loud voices were raised in opposition, and perhaps the most hostile were those of the priests, for some of them even refused absolutions to persons who attended the prior's lectures. These things Savonarola well knew, and therefore looked for but little fruit of his labor in his own day. But from the youths and children who heard him, he hoped much. He delighted in filling their minds with his own healthy thoughts, and often tenderly urged them "to remember his words, and to see that they bore fruit when his voice should be heard no more."

5

Sometimes he told them that in their hands might be placed the guidance and government of their country, the education of children yet unborn. Then, addressing the mothers, he entreated them "to restrain and guide their children as only mothers can. Now he admonished the fathers to secure to their sons the soundest education possible; to assure to them a knowledge of true Christianity, while they acquainted themselves with Virgil, Cicero, and Horace; thus would they acquire both eloquence and the truth."

Great must have been Savonarola's confidence that from his seed-sowing in the hearts of the youthful Florentines a rich harvest would be reaped, for at the close of one of these sermons, we hear him exclaim: "O Florence! deal with me as thou wilt. I have mounted the pulpit this day, to tell thee that thou wilt not destroy my work, because it is the work of Christ. Whether I live or die, the seed I have sown will not the less bear fruit. If my enemies are powerful enough to drive me from thy walls, I shall not be grieved. Some desert I shall find where I can take refuge with my Bible, and enjoy a repose which thy citizens shall not be able to disturb."

Indeed, Savonarola's career proved that with the children his influence was marvelous. Under his gentle, persuasive words and manner, the children of Florence, formerly rude and willful, yielded to his every request. They attended his preaching; joined most heartily with him in the devotional exercises; chanted the sacred songs and hymns which he himself had composed and adapted to music, and which, as he ardently hoped, would induce the older Florentines to discard the pernicious ballads provided by Lorenzo de Medici, to be sung during the annual carnival.

These songs were simply execrable, so odious that, since Savonarola's warfare against them, no one presumed to sing them in the city streets; yet so depraved was the public taste, so vitiated the general opinion, that the "Divina Comedia" of Dante, men presumed to say, was "inferior to the carnival songs of Lorenzo de Medici." Notwithstanding, this was called in Italy "the Golden Age of Literature." To overcome this opinion was fighting one's way up hill; yet upward Savonarola pressed his way undaunted, looking neither to the right hand nor to the left, sure of fruitage from his labor—in the children.

The great man used to say that "a child protected from sin until old enough to exercise self-judgment, acquires so great a purity of heart and mind that the angels of heaven delight to converse with him."

# CHAPTER IX.

## AN EVENT IN FLORENTINE HISTORY.

E shall soon be obliged to present a new phase of Savonarola's life. In order to make this feature plain, we must first glance briefly at an event which now occurred in Florentine history. The period is 1494. Charles VIII. is on the throne of France. Recently, treaties of peace have been made between himself and England, Spain, and Austria. This peace gives him leisure to think about his claim to the crown of Naples. Ludovico il Moro, Duke of Milan, was aware of this claim, and now rashly suggested to Charles that he had better come over and take possession of the little sovereignty. Ludovico had been advised not to take that step, and probably made the proposition little expecting that an attempt in that direction would forthwith follow. But Charles was quite ready for the movement, and so informed the Duke of Milan.

Up to this date, Florence had been on friendly terms with the French king. But, alarmed at the prospect of a foreign army passing through his domain, Pietro de Medici committed the grave mistake of making an alliance with the king of Naples. This made him an enemy of the approaching Charles.

Singularly enough, Italy, the very land to be invaded, encouraged the French expedition, while France herself, aside from the king and court, was

utterly opposed to the undertaking. Nothwith-
standing, on the 5th of September, Charles
crossed the Alps and entered Turin with an army
amazing for the splendor of its infantry, for its
hundreds of spirited Scotch and French cavaliers,
and its many cannon on wheels—a new thing in
that day.

The excitement in Florence rose almost to frenzy,
as rumor after rumor about the invaders reached the
ears of the people. Amid the furor Savonarola
proved to be the only man who could restrain the
fears and feelings of the multitude. He was able to
turn them in whatever direction he pleased, "and
for the next four years the devout prior of San
Marco held the foremost place in Florentine history." His own enthusiasm, deep and glowing, in-
fected everyone who came within his magic influence. A hearty "amen" was the response to
his every opinion or utterance. In short, the man's
power was simply astonishing.

At Brescia, years before, as the reader will remember, Savonarola had foretold that a flood of
frightful calamity would come upon Italy. That
visitation, he now declared, was about to burst upon
the ungodly. The subject of Noah building the
ark furnished him a suitable theme for a series of
sermons on the unrighteous times—"an ark," he announced, " to be constructed, not of gopher-wood,
but of those virtues, the absence of which had
brought the city of Florence to its present degraded
condition."

Plank by plank, the imaginative preacher built
up his unique ark, right before the eyes of the people, an ark in which only those who would repent
were to find refuge. What was to be the nature of
the coming destruction the prior did not indicate as

yet. And as sermon after sermon closed, without
the much-dreaded yet longed-for announcement,
the anxiety of the people became almost insupport-
able. Alluding to that time, Savonarola once said,
" I felt held back from defining what should be the
character of that flood, as by some superior power.

Sunday after Sunday did thousands of people
flock to the Duomo to learn what this disaster was
to be, and went away no wiser than they came.
To hear him, many, coming from a distance in the
country, traveled all night, and at dawn of day were
at the city gates awaiting admission.

"A flood of waters!" Could that be a divine
symbol for the advancing French army?—be that
great chastisement Savonarola had so often referred
to? It must be so; and at their very doors, then,
was the fulfillment of his prediction." Thus believed,
not frightened ignorance only, but learned and
thoughtful men, the profoundest minds in Florence;
for to them was Savonarola's divine mission as
great a reality as to himself. So, with a constant
feeling of awe, did the soberest men of the day
await the descent of the flood upon the corrupt
land, and the still more corrupt church.

Charles' arrival in Turin was unknown in Florence until September 21. That day Savonarola
preached in the Duomo. The church was even
more densely packed than usual. Every jot of space
was occupied hours before the services began. The
anxiety to hear him was intense. At last the mighty
preacher appeared. Amid the deepest silence, with
every eye fastened upon him, he entered the pulpit.
With a calm face he surveyed the great company,
and perceived the ill-suppressed agitation.

The man stood silent for a moment, and then
suddenly, and with loud voice, cried, " Behold! I

bring a flood of waters upon the earth!" Like a terrific thunder-clap, that announcement filled every heart with terror. Savonarola's friend, Prince Pico, who was present, afterwards said: "As I listened, a shudder ran through my frame. The hair of my head stood on end."

Savonarola also admitted that he himself was not less moved than was his audience. In their alarm the people pressed toward the speaker, as if to secure protection from him whose declaration had so moved them. Hitherto had all his prophecies proved true. The three titled ones, whose death he had foretold, were all sleeping in their graves, and now the sword of judgment he had beheld in the air was at the very gates. Not in Florence only, but throughout all Italy, every eye looked to Savonarola for counsel in the emergency. Thus it happened that, as by a stroke of magic, the men attached to him became masters of the city.

In those days of fearful apprehension and danger, the princely ruler of Florence was often seen playing ball in the streets. Not only was Pietro de Medici fierce and tyrannical by nature, but he was utterly incompetent. Not a few now cherished the hope that the march of events would soon end his career as Lord of Florence. Presently information reached the city that Charles and his host were at her very gates! Then flamed forth the suppressed wrath of the people against the weak ruler. He awoke to a sense of his danger. Trembling, stricken with fear, first here, then there, he turned for shelter from the impending catastrophe. There was no shelter; and, "seized by an insane folly, he took the crowning step toward depriving himself of his power."

Pietro called to mind that when his father was at war with Naples five years before, he obtained access to King Ferdinand, and in a personal interview gained peace for Florence and security for himself. He resolved to follow Lorenzo's example, and seek the presence of Charles. Thereupon, without delay, and accompanied by only a few personal friends, he rode forth to Sargano, where the king of France had halted, and there, having secured a safe-conduct, he immediately waited upon the king.

Charles was ready with his requirements, and, frightened out of his wits, Pietro conceded everything, promised the king large sums of money, and ceded to him the strongholds of Pisa and Leghorn. Pleased with having saved his own life, the ignoble prince now rode back to Florence, to present, as an excuse for his traitorous course, the assertion of Charles, that " on no other terms would he promise that his troops should traverse Tuscany as friends and not as foes."

Pietro reached the palazzo publico, in Florence, on the 8th of November. During his absence, indignation over the step he had taken reached a fearful point. His departure from the city was deemed an act which no emergency could justify. Openly, the citizens declared that despotic rule, barely tolerable under Lorenzo, had become unbearable under Pietro—"The Fool." On his way to the palazzo, Pietro received unmistakable evidence of this feeling. Not one of his friends had a word of encouragement, or a word in his defense.

Most dispiritingly, too, some of the leading citizens who had long been firm adherents of the House of the Medici suddenly changed sides, and became bitter foes to the man now bearing that name. An excited multitude, ready to restore liberty to Florence, at almost any cost, filled the palazzo. Advancing through an excited crowd, Pietro reached the place untouched. The Seignory, there assembled, listened to his tale of duplicity without a word of approval. Filled with forebodings, the prince left their presence. Next morning he summoned to his aid five hundred horsemen; but the day had gone by when the proud Florentines could be put down by a few troops.

Every man of the Seignory declared hostility to him; the enraged citizens thirsted for his blood. Pietro made vain attempts to arrest the leaders of the revolution, but was foiled at every step. Escorted by a mounted body-guard, he rode to the great gates of the palazzo, and found them closed. He commanded them to be opened. The Seignory refused to obey. "If he pleased, he could enter alone by the postern, but the gates would not be opened to him."

Thinking discretion the wiser part under the circumstances, Pietro returned to his palace. Barely had he arrived there, when the unmistakable news reached him that, to a man, the Seignory had declared against him, and had pronounced him a rebel and an outlaw. Completely dismayed, he mounted his horse, and, with the cries of "liberty" and "the people" ringing in his ears, passed through the gate San Gallo, and sped away to Bologna.

His brother, Giovanni de Medici, then Cardinal de Nemours, but afterwards Pope Leo X., and the most popular of Lorenzo's sons, addressed the throng from the street. But no effort could avail to stem the tide of antagonism. Showers of stones greeted him from the windows and house-tops. Giovanni, having intrusted a large share of the family treasures to the care of the convent of San Marco, gladly followed his brother to Bologna.

# CHAPTER X.

## CHARLES ENTERS FLORENCE.

T the hour of Pietro's flight, Savonarola was not in Florence. No sooner had the Senate determined to restore the republic, November, 1494, than it dispatched a fresh embassy to King Charles, to arrange for his entering Florence. Savonarola was one of the envoys. It was during his absence that Pietro ingloriously departed.

Before leaving, however, Savonarola preached in the Duomo, and closed his sermon with these solemn words :—

"The Lord has heard your prayers. He has caused a great revolution to end peaceably. When the city was abandoned by its ruler, he alone came to its aid. Persevere, then, O people of Florence! in peace and good works. If you wish the Lord to continue his mercy toward you, be merciful to your enemies. If you be not so, the chastisement preparing for the rest of Italy, will fall upon you. The Lord saith unto you, 'I will have mercy.' Woe to those who disobey the command."

After the sermon, Savonarola set out, on foot, for the French camp.

The other members of the embassage reached Pietra Santa, where Charles now was, a day in advance of the prior. At an audience with the king, they informed him that Florence would give him a friendly reception, if he would enter as a friend. A direct answer Charles would not give. Refusing to

(74)

sign the treaty presented to him, he declined to commit himself to any course of action.

Upon his arrival, Savonarola, alone, entered the royal presence. Wearing the garb of a prior of San Marco, and carrying in his hands the open Gospel, he passed the long line of armed men. Charles, attended by his generals, received him with respect. Pointing to the book, and in a tone of calm authority, Savonarola thus addressed him:—

" Great king! thou minister of divine justice, God has long borne with the grievous sins of Italy, graciously waiting for her repentance. Despite the most sacred obligations, she has lifted up her hard and tawdry face, until now the hour of divine venge-ance is at hand. To his unworthy servant now before thee, God revealed, more than five years ago, his purpose to reform the church by means of severe chastisement. From that time his servant has never ceased to call the people to repentance. This, men of all classes will affirm. Few believed the words spoken; multitudes derided them.

"At length, O king! as the minister of God, the minister of justice, may thine arrival prove alto-gether propitious! But, most gracious king! give ear to my words, and apply them to thy heart. The unworthy servant of God to whom these things have been revealed, admonishes thee that, after his example, thou must in all things incline to mercy, but particularly towards the city of Flor-ence, which, although she has committed great transgressions, yet contains many true servants of God. For their sake thou must preserve the city, that with the more quiet mind we may pray for thee. Therefore, O king! be warned to defend all who need and deserve mercy; but most of all pro-tect thou those devoted to Christ in the nunneries, lest through thee sin should superabound, and the strength given thee from on high be turned into weakness."

Was the character of Charles VIII. such as to encourage Savonarola to expect much compassion from him? Guicciardini thus paints him: "Rash, unstable, uncultivated, young, and good-natured, but one who never considered the consequences of any step he desired to take, and still less regarded his promise, whether extorted from him or voluntarily given, he was unstable as water." Yet Savonarola indulged the hope that his plea had made some impression. Accustomed to sway masses of people, to the degree that they saw with his eyes, believed what he believed, why should he not expect the king to obey his charge?

Unheeded did his grave words fall on the ear of the king. Savonarola was not more successful than his brother ambassadors. Sign a treaty pledging security to Florence, Charles would not. "Everything should be arranged when he reached the great city." This was very little to encourage. Still Savonarola retraced his way, not without hope. He reflected with comfort upon the astonishment Charles evinced, on hearing himself designated as the "rod of God." He did not know how quickly that astonishment gave place to indifference.

On Sunday, November 17, Florence threw open her gates to the French king. "His entry was on a scale of magnificence never before witnessed in that city. As the Florentines assembled upon the streets watched with anxious eye the striking spectacle, the passing Frenchmen heard, here and there, mutterings which presaged no good to the intruders should the populace but get the advantage."

Nevertheless, although large bodies of armed

Florentines lay concealed in the churches and monasteries, ready to spring forth at the slightest provocation, not an act of hostility took place.

Crossing the Ponte Vecchio, Charles proceeded to the Duomo, where he attended divine service, and thence passed on to the palace of the Medici, where splendid preparations had been made for his reception. The magnificence all around them made the invaders feel keenly the wide contrast between the Italian civilization of that period and the comparative lack of luxury in France.

At this juncture there spread through Florence, like wild-fire, a report that Pietro de Medici was at the gates with an armed host. Suddenly the great alarm bell of the palazzo, whose rope was never touched except in hours of peril to Florence, now sent its warning peals through and through the city. Instantly warriors seemed to spring out of the very ground; the streets filled with citizens, and barricades went up as if by magic. The startling rumor proved false, but it demonstrated to the astonished Frenchmen what Florence could do in the line of city barricades when occasion demanded.

At the same hour angry discussion was afoot between Charles and the Senate. The king demanded, first of all, large sums on account of his distressed finances; next, Pietro must be recalled and reinstated; third, for himself he must have the sovereignty of the city. Within her walls a body of men must govern in his name, on the ground that "a conqueror has a right to impose such terms as he pleases upon a conquered people." A conquered people! Florence was not aware that she was conquered, and the assumption brought forth a burst of indignation from the Seignory.

For Florence to free herself of unwelcome guests

by the payment of money, was not a new thing; so
now the large sum required by the monarch was
readily pledged; but before he received it, he must
accede to the terms of a paper now presented. The
terms failed to suit him; whereupon a second con-
tract, drawn by his own advisers, was laid before
the Seignory. The document contained the king's
ultimatum. Its demands were too unjust to be for
a moment considered, and were couched in language so offensive that, stung to the quick, "the
commissioners instantly remonstrated."

Said Charles in reply: "If my terms are not accepted, I shall order my trumpets to sound."

Flaming with anger, Capponi, one of the commissioners, and formerly an ambassador at the court
of France, sprang to his feet, seized the offending
paper from the hand of the secretary, and, tearing it
in pieces, exclaimed: "Sound your trumpets, and
we will ring our bells!"

These were heroic words, and have become immortal. Marvelous was the effect they produced.
Struck dumb with astonishment, both parties re-
emaind silent for a moment. That threat to ring
the bells of Florence did not strike the king favor-
ably. He had just before witnessed the effect of
ringing one bell, and was not anxious to hear more.
Capponi turned to leave the room. Charles called
him back, and took the cutting edge off his threat
to sound the French trumpets, by saying with a
smile: "Ah, Capon! Capon! You are a wicked
Capon!"

At length terms were concluded. They were
ratified in the Duomo, November 26. Fifty thousand ducats were at once transferred to the king's
deplcted treasury. On his part, Charles agreed to
leave the city within two days, and continue his
course to Rome.

# CHAPTER XI.

## THE GREAT PREACHER BECOMES THE POLITICAL ADVISER.

HE time was now the verge of winter. Charles was not eager to cross the Apennines at that season, and suffered day after day to pass without giving any signs of departure. All Florence longed to see him go, for daily altercations were occurring between the citizens and the French soldiery. So, once more, the Senate requested Savonarola to ask audience of the king and urge his leave-taking. Without a moment's hesitation, he consented. Making his way through guards of soldiers, he addressed Charles as one who believed he had for him a message direct from God, saying :—

"Most Christian prince, thy delay here is causing serious mischief, both to our city and to the mission in which thou art engaged. Thou art losing thy time, forgetful of the task imposed upon thee by Providence, to the great detriment of both thy spiritual welfare and thy worldly glory. Listen now to the servant of God. Go on thy way without further delay. Take care that thou dost not bring ruin on this city, and the anger of the Lord upon thyself."

Afterwards, alluding to this interview, Savonarola truly remarked: " I spoke to the king as not one of you would have dared speak, and by the grace of

God he was not offended. I said things which you
yourselves would not have endured, and he patiently
heard them."

Two days after the prior's visit, the king withdrew from Florence. The joy at his departure
was extraordinary. Great numbers flocked to the
churches to thank God most heartily for removing
the scourge which had so sorely chastened them.

The city was now her own mistress, and the
need of an effective form of government, lest the
very liberty she had acquired should destroy her,
grew hourly. And now, for the third time, she
turned to Savonarola for help, and in yielding to
this call, he started the train of circumstances which
led to his ruin.

"Surely, he who had preserved the city from a
deluge of blood after the Medici's flight; he who
had freed them from Charles and his hated troops,
could most safely steer the ship of State." While
preaching in the Duomo, the prior read these
thoughts, it has been said, in the anxious faces
before him, and with the permission of the Senate,
he gave a series of lectures upon the form of government now safest for them.

Having set forth the chief advantages of both
monarchical and popular governments, the preacher
earnestly recommended the latter, as best adapted
to Florentine ideas and character, and as most in
harmony with the traditions of the republic. Naturally, however, the higher class hesitated to trust
the fortunes of the city to a popular government
having the broad basis Savonarola recommended.
Yet, to oppose his plan, supported as it was by the
people, seemed equally hazardous.

There followed many warm debates and tumults.
We cannot here record them. But amid them all,

Savonarola never swerved from the conviction that the only form of government suitable to Florence was a civil and popular one. "Woe be to thee, Florence!" he one day exclaimed from the pulpit, "if thou place at thy head one who shall rule over thee supremely. Tyrant is the name of him who usurps the rights of others. Therefore, your first law should be that no man shall ever have a right to place himself at the head of your city. Such men strive to rise above others, and fail to maintain civil equality. Suffering this, you build upon a bed of sand.

"You know," he continued, "that never willingly have I meddled with the affairs of State, and do you suppose I should now do so did I not see a necessity for my looking into them, for the salvation of your souls? You have seen that my words have come true; that they proceeded not from my own will, but came from God. Listen, then, to one who is seeking only your salvation.

"Pacify your minds; attend to the common good; forget your private interests. Reforming your city by such a course, it will become more glorious than ever. Thus, too, will you begin the reform of Italy, and, spreading your wings over the world, will bring about the reformation of all nations. Forget not that the Lord has given clear signs that he desires the renovation of all things, and that you are the people chosen to begin the good work. Open, O Lord!" he exclaimed, as he finished his appeal, "open, O Lord! the hearts of this people, that they may know the things thou has revealed to me."

Well would it have been for Savonarola had he at this point steadfastly refused to bear any part in the civil affairs of Florence, and had confined himself strictly to the duties of his high calling. In an

6

earlier day he had warmly denounced "princely priests and priestly princes." Both terms imply a union of ecclesiastical and civil affairs,—a union at variance with the spirit and the purity of Christianity,—a union certainly not contemplated by Christ in his commission to his disciples, and one which cannot exist but with detriment to both the church and the State.

That the great Florentine conscientiously undertook to guide the storm-driven barque of civil affairs at Florence, is not to be doubted. That he attempted it solely for the good of the people is instantly to be admitted, for in nothing was Savonarola self-seeking. In everything he was self-denying. Nevertheless, that he made the mistake of his life in so doing, is not to be questioned.

Up to this time his course had been consistent, and his progress continuous and steady; but from this time forward his course was as erratic as that of a ship without a rudder. Hitherto God had been his guide and helper, and his course was right; but henceforth he himself realized that he was wandering as in a maze, having no faithful guide; and yet, strangest of all, he threw upon the Lord all the blame.

The city was indeed now free, but the utmost disorder reigned. Its commerce was ruined; its treasury was drained. Seventy years had it been governed by the rapacious Medici. The art of self-government had been forgotten. There was immense need of a strong guiding mind in complete sympathy with the people. The only such soul in Florence was Savonarola. The love of the Florentines for the great preacher was now mightily increased by his fearless assertion of their rights. They besought him to take the helm. He consented, and without holding the least official position in the commonwealth, became the real head of the State, the actual dictator of Florence.

Now what were his acts ? His first step was to relieve the starving populace within and without the walls. Shops were opened to give work to the unemployed. All taxes, especially those burdening the lower classes, were reduced. The administration of justice was strictly enforced, and constantly in the Duomo all men were urged to put their trust in the Lord.

After much debate over a constitution for the republic, a form of government was drafted after the Venetian plan, with modifications to suit the needs of Florence. Through Savonarola's influence this was adopted. It consisted, first, of a Great Council of thirty-two hundred citizens, over twenty-five years of age, and of blameless reputation, each onethird of whom were to sit six months, in turn, in the great Hall of the Cinquecento, built expressly for the purpose.

Next higher than these was the Council of Eighty. This, with the concurrence of the Senate, was to decide all matters too important and intricate for handling in the larger assembly. This arrangement was submitted to the people, and approved as giving a fair promise of justice.

Savonarola's formula for the action of these councils was : 1. The fear of God and the purification of manners. 2. The promotion of the public welfare before personal interests. 3. A general amnesty to political offenders. 4. No doge, as head of the councils.

Thus, in a very short time—less than one year— had Florence secured many important laws and regulations tending to insure freedom to her people ; and the whole had been effected without the shedding of one drop of blood. To celebrate this victory of liberty over tyranny, and to insure its being never forgotten, a statue of Judith slaying Holofernes was executed by Donatello, and set up at a prominent point in the city. It now stands in a portico of the palace, whither it was removed upon the downfall of the republic. To the magistrates Savonarola said: "Levy taxes only on property, thus putting an end to loans and all arbitrary imposts, cease from strife, love as brethren." Addressing the people, he entreated them to love and assist their fellow-citizens. "A son," he urged, "is under such obligations to his father that he can never do enough for him. Your country is your common father. Every one of you is bound to help it. Were one of you to say, 'I have gained no benefit from it,' you would speak ignorantly."

These and similar exhortations so impressed the Seignory that they often sought counsel of Savonarola at San Marco and in the Palazzo. From that date he was known in Florence as "Il Frate," the brother, and all men bowed to his authority.

His fame for eloquence and oratory was now at its zenith. Day after day his impassioned words, breathing the vehement spirit of the Old Testament prophets, aroused the emotions of the Florentines to a height never before—and never after—experienced by them. Hymns and praises rang in the streets which so recently resounded with the wanton lyrics of Lorenzo. Both sexes dressed in the plainest attire. Mothers nursed their own babes, instead of committing them to other hands. Nobles, scholars, artists, renounced the world to adopt the Dominican gown. Even the laws and edicts of the day read like paraphrases from the sermons of Savonarola.

There are passages in Savonarola's writings which show that, at this hour of wonderful success, he had misgivings as to the consistency of his mingling in the strife and turmoil of political life, and particularly of dealing with such matters in the pulpit. And more strangely still, he seems to have soon satisfied himself that in this, as in other things, he was but bowing to the manifest will of God. Listen to the fervid outpouring of his mind on this point :—

"I have said: Lord, thou art just, good, almighty. Thou art my God. Out of nothing hast thou created me. I am but dust and ashes, yet with confidence will I speak to thee, for thou hast been crucified for me. Pardon me if I am too familiar in my speech. Lord, thou who directest all things well, thou hast deceived me; thou hast betrayed me worse than man was ever betrayed; because, though I have long time prayed that thou wouldst grant me such grace that I might never be compelled to aid in the government of others, thou hast ordered just the reverse.

"Little by little hast thou drawn me into the snare. Had I seen the snare, perhaps I had not been what I am. As the moth which desires the light when it sees the burning candle, not knowing that it burns, singes its wings, so have I done. Thou hast shown me thy light, in which I rejoice greatly, and having told me that it is well to make manifest thy light for the salvation of men, I have plunged into the fire and burned the wings of contemplation. I have entered a vast sea, and with great desire I long for the haven, but I see no way to return.

"Oh! my sweet haven, shall I ever find thee more! Oh, my heart, how hast thou ever suffered thyself to be drawn away from thy sweet haven! Oh, my soul, look where thou art! Surely we are in the midst of a deep sea, and the winds are adverse on every side. Lord, I say unto thee, as Jeremiah said: 'Lord, thou hast deceived me and I was deceived. Thou art stronger than I and hast prevailed. I am in derision daily. Everyone mocketh me, for I cried out; I cried violence and spoil, because the word of the Lord was made a reproach unto me and a derision daily.'

"And again will I say with Jeremiah: 'Woe is me, my mother, that thou hast borne me a man of strife, a man of contention to the whole earth.' I would go to the haven and I find not the way. I seek rest, but no place of rest can I find. I would be at peace and speak no more; but at peace I cannot be, for the word of the Lord is as a fire in my heart. His word, if I utter it not, burns my bones and my marrow. Well then, Lord, if thou wilt that I navigate this deep sea, thy will be done!"

At the end of this changeful year, 1494, Savonarola's sermons began to be directly and confessedly political. Not that they ceased to set forth the subject of religion; this they never failed to do. But the political took precedence of the religious element in them; and upon political success was made largely to depend the success of religion.

# CHAPTER XII.

OME of the greatest historians and states-
men of Savonarola's time regarded the constitution he framed for Florence as the very
best that could have been devised. Said Sig-
nor Villari: "To fully understand the part he took
in its construction, we must follow up every step
taken with reading the sermons he preached from
day to day during the period. And we must also
follow the debates still preserved in the journals of
the proceedings, in the archives of the Seignory at
the palace. Therein do the citizens use the friar's
very language, and adduce his very arguments to
such a degree that one might consider their speeches
mere repetitions of his sermons. Only after having
done this are we aware of the extent to which this
man became the informing soul of the republic."

The new laws were written in Italian instead of
Latin, as was the custom during the reign of the
Medici. This was done that all the people might be
able to read and understand the laws by which they
were governed. "In many instances they were
extracts almost *verbatim* from the prior's sermons."

About the close of 1495, the condition of Florence was such as to call forth the highest praise
from Savonarola and the councils. Machiavelli,
the shrewd but skeptical Florentine secretary, a
man not likely to overestimate one so incomprehen-
sible to him as the zealous and unselfish prior of
San Marco, many times alludes to "the learning,
prudence, and purity of his mind, ever breathing

(87)

divine virtue," and says, "Of such a man one ought never to speak but with reverence."

But it is Guicciardini who observes of Savonarola and the new government: "Such was the love of the Florentines for the liberties bestowed upon them in 1494, that no arts, no soothings, no cunning devices of the Medici, ever made them forget it." He informs Florence: "You are under heavy obligations to the friar, who not only arrested the tumult in good time, but accomplished that which without him could have been accomplished only through great disorders and bloodshed."

Of that highly dramatic era, eminent modern writers also have spoken in the most laudatory words. Francesco Forte, an Italian versed in the affairs of his country, remarks: "The reforms introduced by the friar constituted, perhaps, the most just government Florence ever enjoyed in her days as a republic! Italy can boast of few greater men than Savonarola, and perhaps not one as great in the political history of the Florentine republic."

But we are most concerned to know what was the state of Savonarola's own mind in this hour of eminent success. What were his reflections as he looked out upon the Florence he had rescued? Was he exultant? Did he break out into rejoicings? Could we but see him in his cell, alone with his God, we should behold a man bowed under a strong conviction of impending evil, soon to break upon both Florence and himself. Hear his sad words:—

"I am wearied, O Florence, by my four years of increasing discourses, which have only exhausted myself, while laboring for you. I have been afflicted with the thought, never absent from my mind, of the scourge I see approaching, and of the dangers to which it will expose you, if you do not turn to the Lord. I pray continually that the joyful be not changed into sorrowful auguries."

It had become his settled conviction that he should die a violent death. Frequently he mentioned it. Barely had the Great Council been established—that institution "called forth in obedience to the will of God," as he said—when, of a Sunday morning, the great cathedral was crowded by thousands expecting to hear a sermon full of praise and triumphant thanksgiving. Did a single such sentence fall from his lips? Once more hear him:—

"A young man, leaving his father's house, went to fish in the sea. The master of the vessel took him far out on the deep; from thence he could no longer discern the port, and thereupon he began to utter lamentations." Then the great leader looked thoughtfully around upon the vast throng for a moment, and cried: "O Florence! that youth is now before you. I left my father's house to find the harbor of religion, in pursuit only of liberty and a quiet life—two things I loved above all others. I was then but twenty-three years old. But when I began to gain some courage, and to find peace in preaching, the Lord led me upon the sea, and carried me far out upon the deep, where now I am.

"I can no longer descry the harbor. I see before me threatening tempests and tribulations. The wind is driving me farther out. On my right are the elect, calling upon me for help. On my left are demons and the wicked, tormenting and raging. Above me I see everlasting goodness, and thitherward hope encourages me. I see beneath me hell, which, from human frailty, I must dread, and into which, but for the help of God, I must fall. O Lord, whither hast thou led me?

"I am so fixed that I can no more return to the quiet I have left. Why hast thou created me to live among the discords of the earth? Once was I free. Now am I the slave of everyone. From

every side I see war and disorder coming upon me.
But do you, O my friends! have pity upon me.
Flowers are good works. Give me flowers. I wish
for nothing more than that you should do what is
acceptable to God."

꜒ Greatly agitated, Savonarola paused for a moment, then said, " Now let me have some rest in
this tempest." Then, recovering himself, he exclaimed : " But what, what, O Lord, shall be the
reward in the life to come, for those who have
come out of such a fight victorious!—It will be
that which eye hath not seen, nor ear heard—eternal beatitude. But what is to be the reward in this
present life ? ' The servant will not be greater than
his master,' is the answer of the Lord. 'Thou
knowest that after I had taught, I was crucified, and
thus thou wilt suffer martyrdom.' "

"O Lord! Lord!" he then cried, in tones that
rang through the Duomo, terrifying every heart in
the vast audience; "grant me this martyrdom!
Let me quickly die for thy sake, as thou hast died
for me! Already I see the ax sharpened. But the
Lord bids me, ' Wait yet awhile, until that be finished which must come to pass, and then shalt
thou show that strength of mind which shall be
given unto thee.' " There was a pause, when Savonarola solemnly exclaimed, " Praise the Lord
for his goodness!" and resumed his discourse.

When we come to review the circumstances at-
tending Savonarola's death, we shall see that this
simple allegory, in which he represents himself as
out upon the deep, with demons and the wicked
raging around him, is almost a photograph of some
of the actual scenes. In view of the facts it seems
almost prophetic.

# CHAPTER XIII

## THE ENMITY OF THE POPE.

IN January of this year, 1495, Pope Alexander VI. became much annoyed over a sermon of Savonarola's, in which he compared the church to a fig-tree, which "in its early days produced abundant fruit and no leaves, but after lapse of years, as many leaves as figs, and later still, leaves only. And not only was this tree fruitless, but its overshadowing foliage injured the neighboring plants." This unhappy condition of affairs appeared to move the prior's heart to its very depths. "You cannot doubt," he said, earnestly addressing his audience, "that the gardener will cut down so useless a tree and condemn it to the flames." Then, no longer using the illustration, he said with great effect :—

"Thus is it with the church. In primitive times she yielded abundant fruit, and as it were, no leaves; but she has grievously degenerated, and now bears leaves only—fruit none. In other words, outward ceremonies abound; pomp and luxury are everywhere, leading men into every error. Just as the heavy foliage of the fig-tree ruins the adjoining plants, so the prelates of the church corrupt other souls by their evil example. But this state of things will not last forever. The husbandman, that is, Christ, will come and cut down the tree; will renew and reform the church."

Here Savonarola paused, and after a moment, in profound accents, said: "When Pope Innocent

VIII. died, I was laughed at for declaring that the
church must be reformed. But at that very time
a vision was granted me. I beheld a black cross
suspended over Babylonian Rome. Upon it was
inscribed, 'The wrath of the Lord.' Around the
cross gleamed swords, lances, arms of all kinds,
while there fell hail, lightning, and hot thunder-
bolts. Then I saw another cross. It was of gold,
and reached to heaven. It hovered over Jerusalem,
and bore this inscription, 'The mercy of God.'
Surrounding it was a serene, limpid, and pure
atmosphere. From that vision I learn that a reformation of the church is not only needed, but
is at hand."

The instant effect of that sermon at the Vatican
was an order commanding Savonarola to preach the
Lent sermons at Lucca, probably with the intent of
getting the preacher away from the reach of his
friends, but by request of the Senate the order was
withdrawn, and the prior remained in the city.

The reader will recall Savonarola's early enemy
at Florence—Mariano Gennezzano. The man was
now at Rome, and gladly improved the opportunity that fact gave him, of feeding the enmity
which daily increased in the heart of Alexander
against this daring accuser of the church, whom
he styled "the tool of the devil." Affairs proceeded, and on July 25, 1495, Savonarola received
the subjoined letter from His Holiness.

"MUCH-LOVED SON: Health and apostolic benediction. We hear that among all the laborers in
the Lord's vineyard, you show the most zeal.
This greatly delights us, and we give praise for it
unto Almighty God. We have also heard that
you affirm that your declarations concerning
future events do not proceed from yourself, but
from God; and therefore, in accordance with the

duties of our pastoral office, we would converse with thee and thereby know more especially what is pleasing to God. Therefore, we exhort you that, in the spirit of all holy obedience, you come to us without delay, who will receive you with love and charity."

Before replying to this wily letter, Savonarola preached a remarkable sermon in the Duomo, in which he warned the people of dangers threatening the republic, especially from the Arrabbiati, and from Pietro de Medici, who was plotting a scheme for his return to Florence.

The church was thronged. Dispirited and apprehensive, weak and trembling, he ascended the pulpit. He had much to say to Florence, for he was about to leave the city for awhile, to regain strength. Among the matters which sorely troubled him was the failure of Charles VIII. to fulfill the mission on which, as Savonarola firmly believed, God had brought him into Italy—that of being, first, the instrument of punishment to the country, and then its restorer to a nobler condition. This omission, the prior well knew, gave tempting occasion to the unbelievers in his own divine mission, to plot for his downfall, and through that for the overthrow of the republic.

No sooner, however, had he begun to speak than he seemed to be animated by a sudden baptism of the Spirit, and poured forth a torrent of fearless condemnation of vice, and declaration of judgment to come, upon those who wickedly should disturb the peace of Florence. The sermon was replete with advice upon practical affairs. At its close he took leave of his hearers in this singular manner:—

"My people, when I am in this pulpit, I feel myself to be in a sound state; and could I con-

tinue to feel so when absent from it, I should ever
be strong. But I leave it now to attend to my
health. It will be some time before I see you
again. If I live, I shall resume preaching. During
my absence, Fra Domenico will preach. I think I
must rest for a month, unless your prayers restore
me sooner. And now I must conclude, for I have
preached until I am quite exhausted, and thus
have shortened my life by many years." Then,
ceasing to address his audience, he suddenly asked:
"Well, then, friar, what reward do you wish to
receive?" "I wish to receive martyrdom. I am
willing to undergo it. I pray for it daily," was his
unhesitating reply.

Many similar tragic declarations did the highly
imaginative Dominican utter between this date and
his sad end. One cannot but question the wisdom
of them. That very day men listened to his
avowal that he wished for martyrdom who were
not the least unwilling his desire should be gratified, and yet who, up to that moment, perhaps,
had not thought of such a death for the dictator
of Florence. Moreover, in the pontifical chair at
Rome, sat one who was not likely to deny the
privilege of martyrdom to any aspirant for the
favor. In the end he was but too delighted to
honor Savonarola in this respect.

Three days after this discourse, the prior replied
to the Pope's letter. We append a few sentences,
which indicate its tone throughout. Savonarola
informed his holiness that he " had long desired to
visit Rome, especially that he might tread where
had walked St. Peter and St. Paul. But many ob-
stacles stood in the way of the accomplishment of
this wish—causes anyone must consider reasona-
ble. His bodily infirmity and agitation of mind,
caused by overexertion in behalf of the State, was

chief among them. In obedience to the command of his physician, he had determined to omit preaching and all severe study for a while."

Finally, referring to dangers which at times had threatened him, he continued: "Although I place my trust in the Lord, I consider that I ought not to tempt him by omitting due caution, even as it is written, 'If they persecute you in one city, flee ye into another.'" Then he calls the magnate's attention to a "little book he has lately written, which will inform him in reference to his preaching upon the events which would bring ruin upon the country, and then renovation of the church."

In Florence there existed at this time three political parties, which we now find it needful to define. First, there were the Piagnoni, the steadfast friends of Savonarola, and the fervent advocates of liberty. They were the largest and most powerful body. As one man they were united in restoring the republic and in opposing the popular vices. They exerted vast influence from this time until the close of the Florentine commonwealth. Peculiar and plain in dress, they were everywhere easily recognized. Stern in manners, strict in discipline, their only weapons of warfare were prayer and the sermons of Savonarola.

The Arrabbiati constituted the second faction. They embraced the higher class only, and were distinguished for excesses in every abominable vice. They opposed equally Savonarola and the Medici. An oligarchy was their beau ideal of a government. Their hatred of the austere Piagnoni was of course bitter. For their rigid morals and democratic principles, Arrabbiati contempt was supreme.

The third and weakest order, called the Bigi, included the Medici and their adherents. Usually, though not always, the Piagnoni and the Bigi united in opposing the Arrabbiati.

It startles us to learn that even while Savonarola was answering the Pope's letter, the corrupt Arrabbiati were scheming to silence forever his offending tongue. This fact, with utter distrust of Alexander's affectionate lines, made the Piagnoni tremble for the prior's safety, should he leave Florence. They believed that, should he even start for Rome, he would be either snatched up on the way, or be tendered the hospitalities of a dungeon in the castle of St. Angelo the moment he entered the gates of the city. Therefore his illness was a cause of sincere rejoicing to his friends.

Matters rested until September, 1495, when the Pope, still mindful of his victim, sent to the friars of Santa Croce, in Florence, a brief, mentioning " a certain friar Girolamo, a disseminator of false doctrines." From Santa Croce the brief was forwarded to Savonarola. This was but a step in the Pope's plan. He knew well that the prior of San Marco was a Dominican, not a Franciscan, and he also knew that the two orders were not on good terms, and to promote his own schemes, thus fanned the fire of ill-will.

Of this artful paper Savonarola wisely took no notice, but, alluding to it shortly before his death, he asked: "Why was it addressed to the monastery of Santa Croce while intended for San Marco? And why did it mention ' a certain Girolamo,' as if he were not well known?"

In October he resumed his pulpit labors. The first three sermons were like shells thrown into the Medician camp, and demolished Pietro's project for re-entering Florence. Their effect was felt in Rome also, for on November 4 came a decisive command from the Pope to cease entirely from preaching.

To Savonarola the evidently growing hostility of Alexander was a deep affliction. To become the

opponent of the head of the church was to occupy
a position from which his very soul drew back.
And amid the conflicting circumstances he was not
quite sure of his path. But, whatever might be the
issue to himself, the church of Christ must not suffer. Therefore he obeyed. But in a short time he
was putting forth all his strength, together with the
cardinal of San Pietro, in Vincoli—afterward Pope
Julius II.—toward convening a council to depose
Alexander, whose election, all Italy knew, had been
carried only by bribery.

To call this council seems to have been the duty,
or the office, of King Charles, who was rather dis-
posed to comply with the cardinal's hot pleading
for the step; for Guicciardini records that, when
Charles passed through Rome during his invasion
of Italy, not less than eighteen cardinals were long
closeted with him, discussing the measure, and also
that ever-crying need, church reform, Julius himself
being one of the conclave. But the king never
came to the point of incurring the responsibility,
and the council never was called.

At this trying period Savonarola's brother Borso
died. To his mother this was a severe stroke. It
called forth from Savonarola a letter to her, expressed in a charming way. There was no one
upon the earth so dear to him as his mother. How
keenly, then, must it have tried him to close his
letter with this announcement, after recurring to
Florentine affairs: " I feel sure that my death is not
far distant, and I would that your faith were so
strong that, like the holy Hebrew woman, of whom
we read in the Old Testament, you might look with
dry eyes upon your son's suffering and martyrdom
before your eyes. My dearest mother, I have not
thus written to pain you, or in forgetfulness of your
grief, but in order that, should it happen to me as
I expect, you may be prepared for it all."

# CHAPTER XIV.

THE Pope's interdict of Savonarola's preaching was withdrawn just before Lent, 1496, and on the 17th of February he preached the first of his famous discourses of that season. Almost simultaneously, with the advice of an influential Dominican bishop, Alexander tendered the prior of San Marco a cardinal's hat, with the suggestion that he modify somewhat the tone of his sermons. "Come to my next sermon, and you shall hear my reply to Rome," was his fearless answer; and on the following Sunday, in tones of thunder, he proclaimed from the cathedral pulpit: "I will have no hat but one dyed with my blood."

Not long was this answer in traveling to Rome, and through all Italy. And everybody now knew that henceforth a deadly conflict would exist between the humble monk and the occupant of the chair of St. Peter. Day after day throngs filled the Duomo, eager to hear the voice which Rome could silence only in death. Multitudes could not gain entrance to the church. Not only men and women but hosts of children came to listen.

These were the children who, at the May festival preceding—only because the great man asked it— had collected money for the poor; had sung his sweet hymns instead of the impure ballads of Lorenzo de Medici; had given up their cruel custom of throwing stones, whereby always some citizens lost their lives, and had turned the last great day of the carnival into a blessing—because the friar wished it; because he had said: "God loves you, and you ought not to grieve him by doing any wrong thing."

Savonarola loved the children; was glad they came to hear him; and hoped they would hear that which they would never forget. So within the great Duomo were erected for these children seventeen rows of seats, leading up to the first row of windows. Here they sat, quiet and very attentive. Often did the man whose words were stirring all Italy turn to these children, and, addressing them, utter teachings they could understand.

Never had his words produced such effect as now, on friend or foe, and repeated were the plots to assassinate him on the way to or from the cathedral. But armed friends in homely garb surrounded him. Blows aimed at him must first strike them. One with him they were in spirit and purpose of life, and never were friends more devoted. They were the Piagnoni.

Artists of every class were among the attendants during this Lent,—painters, sculptors, architects, engravers,—all of highest renown. "For eight consecutive years was Fra Bartolommeo ever to be seen in his seat," listening, absorbed, to words cherished to the last hour. Bartolommeo, celebrated especially for the refined beauty of his Madonnas, was but twenty-three years old when he began to attend the prior's services. He loved to depict sacred subjects, and was engaged in painting a fresco—the Last Judgment—in the church of San Marco, when Savonarola preached a mighty sermon on the iniquity of the day. No class escaped his scathing words. Like the edge of a sword they cut Pope and peo-

ple, the Medici, the affluent Florentines, any who
debased art.

Bartolommeo, sadly perplexed by this sermon,
never added another touch to his Last Judgment.
True, he loved what was pure and beautiful in art,
but some of his works were of the class unsparingly
condemned by the preacher. These, every one, he
destroyed, and warmly united with Savonarola in
his desire to reform art. This great painter was
one of the hundreds of citizens who, for the defense
of the prior, made their way to San Marco on that
long-remembered day when the Arrabbiati besieged the convent, and with frightful cries demanded that Savonarola be given up to them.

That 17th of February, to which we have referred,
was a grave and momentous day. Savonarola knew
that the series of discourses would add tenfold to
Alexander's wrath. Before the hour for him to
leave the cloister, the Seignory dispatched officers
to guard the way to the Duomo. Instantly, upon
his leaving his cell, his body-guard closed around
him. He reached the cathedral in safety. Thousands awaited him. Slowly, as if weak in body, he
climbed the pulpit stairs. But once in the loved
spot, he was strength itself. Slowly surveying the
audience, his eyes glowing like living coals, he
stood a moment deeply moved, and then began his
discourse in the form of a dialogue with himself.

But soon dropping this style, he stated that, having carefully examined all his teachings, he had
reached the firm conviction that he had "taught
only what the holy Catholic Church believes," notwithstanding his doctrine had been so obnoxious to
the Pope. Then he boldly announced that he was
not bound to obey the commands of ecclesiastical
superiors, "not even those of the Pope, if they are

contrary to charity or the gospel." " I believe," he
continued, "the Pope would not wish me to do so,
but should he, I should reply: 'Thou art not a
good shepherd. Thou art in error.'

"As to my not obeying the order to come to
Rome," he explained, " I did not consider myself
bound to obey a command which the whole city of
Florence, down to the simplest maiden, knew proceeded from political hatred. Did I think my
leaving Florence would be for its good, I would
willingly go; but not believing this, I will not obey
the order of any living man."

During this series of sermons, to be the most
famous of his life, Savonarola proposed to consider
a wide range of topics, and in this initial one, he
touched upon most of these themes. And throughout the discourse, the independence of his utterances amazed friend and foe. His words were
aflame with truth and courage. Never had he
spoken anything at all comparable to the opinions
he now expressed.

At one point he burst out with the question: " I
ask thee, Rome, how is it possible that thou canst
still exist? By night thy priests are sunk in the
lowest depths of vice. Next morning they read
mass and celebrate the sacraments. At Rome all
is venal. Every position is put up for sale. Even
the blood of Christ is to be had for money." Then,
turning to the audience, he said:—

"Ye are corrupt in everything; in your speaking and in your silence; in what you do, in what
you do not do; in your belief and your unbelief.
You declaim against prophecy. Yet someone tells
you a strange dream, and you believe him. You
fast on a certain Saturday, under the belief that
you will be saved. I tell you, the Lord desires not

either certain days or certain hours, but that in
every day of your life you should flee from sin.
But you are good one hour of the day that you
may be wicked the rest of your lives.  See what
took place during the last three days of Holy Week
—such running after indulgences and  pardons!
such kissing of the images of St. Peter and St. Paul,
of this saint and of that! such coming and going,
ringing of bells, decking out of altars, and adorning
of altars!   All this for three days before Easter, but
no longer.   God is indifferent to these your doings,
because you will be more wicked after  Easter than
before."

A little later in the series, he electrified his hearers by exclaiming: "What if I should ask you to
give me ten ducats for the poor!  You would not.
But should I command, 'Lay out an hundred ducats on  the chapel of San Marco,' you would.  Yes,
not for the honor of God, but for putting up there
your armorial bearings!  Look around the convents.   You see their walls covered with coats-of-
arms.   Upon looking up at what is over the door
of the convent, I fancied  I should see a crucifix,
and it was a coat-of-arms!   Once more I look up,
and again  a  coat-of-arms.   Nothing else is to be
seen.   I observe some drapery, and conclude it cov-
ers the painting of a crucifix, but I find a coat-of-
arms.   These, these are the idols to whom your
sacrifices are offered."

Each of these sermons, as we might expect,
prophesied vehemently of coming evil.  Savonarola
repeatedly assured his auditors that a terrible pestilence would desolate Florence.  "Be assured," he
said, "there will not be left here people enough to
bury the dead, and there will be no means for having numerous burials.  So many deaths will there

be that men will go through the streets, crying
with loud voice: 'Who has any dead? Who has
any dead?' And people will run out of their homes
saying: 'Here is my son; here is my brother;
here is my husband.' So thinned will the population become that very few will remain."

One can readily imagine the effect of such predictions. And in such an age, its almost immediate
fulfillment was necessary to awaken confidence in
the prophet. Otherwise there would be aroused
against him a very frenzy of indignation, which only
his blood could allay.

Ere this Lent closed, the new hall for the "Great
Council" was completed, and to the occasion Savonarola devoted two of his sermons. They were
confined exclusively to political affairs, and certainly were replete with advice worthy to be
adopted by any state, in any age. The place of
meeting was transferred from the Duomo to the
Great Hall. Seventeen hundred persons convened
to hear him, and everything conspired to render
the event one of lively joy to the prior. It was
February 25, 1496. Referring, among other topics
of interest, to that of the Florentine elections, he
heartily denounced the party spirit they had previously excited, together with the custom of circu-
lating hand-bills in which certain persons were denounced as unfit for official positions. "You ought,"
he said, "to pay no regard to these hand-bills. If
you have good reason to believe that a candidate is
a bad man, say so openly. Frankly declare your
opinion that such a man is not the right one for the
office proposed for him. But if he be a right man,
elect him." Directly addressing the Piagnoni, he
said:—

"I fear some of the council have said of a cer-

tain candidate, 'He is a friend of the friar, let us
give him a black bean ' "—a black bean in the Florentine elections stood for an affirmative vote.  "Is
this  the  lesson  I  have  taught you?—My  only
friends are Christ and he who does what is right.
Such a course will immediately create divisions.
Let every elector give his vote to whomsoever, in
his conscience, he believes to be a good and pru-
dent man."

If these words of the actual, but not official,
dictator of Florence were honest words—and who
can say they were not?—they were the words of an
incorruptible patriot.  No spirit of self-seeking
tainted his motives.  For the welfare of Florence,
and at the call of God, as he persuaded himself,
Savonarola—though the doing so grieved his in-
most soul—would try to serve both church and
state, sadly forgetting that the great Head of the
church himself had said, " Ye cannot serve two
masters."

It is remarked that every person who bore any
part in the construction of that vast hall was an
adherent of Savonarola.  Its erection was super-
vised by Cronaca, a celebrated architect of that day.
Michael Angelo was among the first conferred with
in reference to it, and an altar-piece was painted for
it by Fra Bartolommeo.  At first it grew but slowly.
Finally certain pulpit talks of Savonarola incited
Cronaca to greater effort, and so remarkable now
was his progress that observers remarked, " The
angels have come to assist him."

The effect of these Lent sermons moved the
Florentines wonderfully.  Thereupon Savonarola
thought he might carry out any plan he chose to
adopt.  Palm Sunday was drawing nigh, and he determined to arrange for a procession of children on

that day. It was a parade of boys only. Eight
thousand formed the impressive spectacle. They
were the material upon which Savonarola built his
hopes for the future of Florence. "The clergy and
monks of the various orders, in full canonicals, followed the boys, and after them a vast multitude of
citizens—men and women, old and young, rich and
poor. A great company of young girls robed in white
and crowned with garlands of snowy flowers—their
mothers accompanying them—closed the procession.
As it moved along, hymns were chanted, patriotic
songs were sung, and the bells pealed forth their
joyous tones."

Arrived at the Duomo, Savonarola tenderly addressed the children some time, and closed the exercises with an urgent appeal to the people of Florence to "accept Christ as their king." And here
the great prior of San Marco forgot that Christ had
declared, "My kingdom is not of this world."

But a little subsequent to this event, when speaking of the perpetuity of the church, he once more
alluded to his own death, which he felt assured was
just at hand, saying, as if to himself: "What then
will be the end of the war you are keeping up?
If you ask me what will be the general end, I answer, VICTORY! But if you ask what will be the end
to me in particular, I answer, DEATH. *Death* but
not *extinction*. Death first, resurrection afterward.
Rome shall not quench this fire, as she will try to
do; if she quenches it for a time, another and
stronger fire will break out. I am but an instrument in the hand of the Lord. I am determined to
fight to the last."

Amos and Zechariah furnished the texts for the
sermons of this Lent. Far and wide did their fame
spread. The Sultan at Constantinople ordered

them to be translated into the Turkish language
that he himself might read them. No previous
efforts of the friar had produced such an impression.
His enemies were simply furious, while the devotion of his friends exceeded all bounds. Alexander
was enraged. The princes of Italy strongly condemned them; those of Germany eagerly read them.
Into France and England also they made their way.
We have mentioned Colet, the Oxford reformer, as
one who listened to Savonarola's preaching about
this time. It is quite certain that he was in Italy in
1496, and more than probable that he heard these
thrilling Lent sermons. With the Piagnoni they
increased his esteem many fold. Il Moro, Duke of
Milan, one of the wounded princes, called forth
from the misrepresented preacher this reply, " I
allude to all persons, to none individually."

When the infuriated Borgia—Pope Alexander
VI.—was reminded that he had given the prior permission to resume preaching, he retorted: " Well,
well, we will not now talk about Friar Girolamo.
Erelong there will be a fitter opportunity." To
hasten this "opportunity," he soon convened a
consistory of fourteen Dominicans to investigate
Savonarola's conduct and doctrines, that he might
find whereof to accuse him. Thirteen of these com-
passionate brethren found him guilty—of what?—
" Of being the cause of all the evil that had befallen
the house of Medici!"

Soon another fatal step was taken. During this
year, 1496, was formed what is known in Italian
history as "The Holy League." The parties to
the alliance were Alexander VI.; Maximilian, king
of the Romans; Ferdinand and Isabella, of Spain;
Henry VII., of England; the Siegnory of Venice,
and Il Moro, Duke of Milan The design of this

league was "the maintenance of the rights of the
Holy Roman Empire and the Papal See, and the
defense and preservation of the separate parties."
From this coalition Florence kept clear, adhering
to her French ally, Charles VIII. This decision
brought herself and Savonarola—her adviser—into
the position of conspirators against Rome, Naples,
Milan, and the Pope above all others. On the 31st
of July, the conditions of the league were published simultaneously in Rome, Naples, and Venice.
At Venice they were proclaimed in the great church
of St. Mark. High mass was celebrated by the
patriarch. For three days the bells were rung and
bonfires were lighted.

In the midst of this turmoil, the man conspicuous
above all others in Italy, calmly wrote his com-
mentary upon the eightieth psalm. He preached
less frequently now, but when he did, his themes
were drawn from the books of Ruth and Micah.
On one occasion, upon entering the pulpit of the
Duomo, he exclaimed: "Here we are still. We
have not fled. I cannot exist without preaching,
and am come in obedience to Him who is Prelate
of prelates and Pope of popes." Then he earnestly
besought the Lord to send his Holy Spirit down
upon the church.

About this date the Seignory requested him to
preach before the magistrates and chief citizens.
He took the occasion to review his past life, and to
refute the charges constantly brought against him,
saying:—

"My enemies go about crying: 'The friar wants
money. He has secret correspondence'—meaning,
probably, with the Medici—'The friar wants a cardinal's hat.' I tell you that if such were the case,
you would not now see me with a ragged cloak."

Then, addressing the Divine One, he cried : " I wish
to glorify myself in thee and in thee alone.   I wish
neither miter nor hat.   I desire that only which
thou hast bestowed upon the saints—death."

In September a brief was issued by the Pope,
annexing the Convent of San Marco to the vicarate
of Lombardy, thus placing the contumacious friar
under control of the vicar-general of the Lombard Congregation, and requiring him to submit
meekly to his authority, to go wherever ordered,
and to " abstain from preaching both in public and
private."   At a glance Savonarola saw the object
of this union of convents.   If the Congregation of
San Marco were dissolved, his authority as friar
would necessarily cease.   And if, in obedience to
the Pope, he left Tuscany—"go wherever he was
sent"—he should inevitably fall into the hands of
Alexander Borgia.

In reply he "regretted that the Holy Father had
been so deceived with regard to him.   As to doctrines, he had preached only what the church
taught.   And respecting prophecy, he had never ex-
plicitly claimed to be a prophet.   It would not be
heresy if he had.   He had indeed predicted many
things.   Some had come to pass, others would.
But to remit their cause to the Lombard Congregation, would be to abandon them to the adversary;
for, as everybody knew, controversy existed between
the two congregations.   In conclusion, he prayed
His Holiness to grant him "an answer and full absolution," adding that he was "willing to submit
himself and his writings to the correction of the
Holy Roman Church."

Here again Savonarola's inconsistency palpably
appears.   In the pulpit of the Duomo, where
hundreds could hear his defiant words, he nobly

asserts that he will "submit to no man," he will "fight to the end;" but in the silence of his cell at San Marco, with none but the Pope to read, he craves full absolution from papal lips, submits his works to the correction of the church, which really means submitting them to the Pope.

Still, from his letter the shrewd Alexander must have inferred that Savonarola would neither dissolve his congregation of convents, nor himself leave Florence. So he made the best of the situation, and in a reply dated October 16, expressed his "joy at the recovery of the lost sheep," adding: "We have in other letters manifested our grief over those tumults in Florence, of which thy sermons have been the chief cause, for, instead of preaching against vice and urging union, you have announced future events—a course sure to create discord, especially in Florence, where the seeds of faction are so thickly sown. For these reasons you have been pressed to come to Rome. But now we are fully persuaded that our good son has erred more from oversimplicity than from an evil mind."

Then followed the repeated command "to abstain from preaching, in public and private, so that none might say his church had been turned into a conventicle." After which he expressed his "earnest longing to behold his beloved son in the holy city, and promised him a joyful reception."

Did these velvet words deceive Savonarola?— Not in the least. He knew exactly what estimate to place on all the Pope's paternal expressions. Barely had this letter arrived, when there came a document from the Florentine ambassador at Rome, announcing that the Pope toiled night and day to accomplish the friar's death.

# CHAPTER XV.

HE close of the year 1496 was freighted with events trying to Savonarola, and threatening to the peace of Florence. The Pope's bull of September 16, commanding the friar to cease preaching altogether, was quickly followed by the papal letter of October 16, reiterating the injunction. Naturally, these papers caused long and painful thought on the part of Savonarola, and deep anxiety in the minds of his friends. Should he resist these commands, or be silent? Himself only considered, he would resist them, but he could not bring reproach upon the church. The bare thought of that was misery to him. For the present, at least, he would be quiet.

About this time, the king of the Romans—urged to the step by Venice and Milan, in the hope that Florence would thus be forced to join the Holy League of which we have spoken—threatened to invade Italy. Florence expended vast sums of money in preparations to repel him. Happily, a depleted treasury kept Maximilian at home. Great was the delight of Florence over her escape from war. Manifestly, the divine hand had saved her. But scarcely had the horrors of invasion been averted, ere famine was at the door. Daily the supply of food diminished. Ships laden with corn for the relief of the city, were detained by contrary winds. And now in the streets of Florence was

(110)

heard the predicted cry: "Bring out your dead."
Famished women and tender children died by the
roadside. Misery made all faces wan and pale; rich
and poor suffered alike. Over all this agony the
Arrabbiati rejoiced. The calamity would prove to
Florence that her great prophet was false. She
had not prospered.

In such an extremity what was Savonarola's
duty? Urged by the Seignory, and by his compassion for the people burning like a fire within
him, he set the papal mandate at defiance and
appeared in the pulpit of the Duomo. How great
was the change six weeks had made in his audience! Many were the vacant seats. The dejected
air of those present spoke of suffering and hunger.
In the audience were numbers of the Arrabbiati.
Savonarola read their thoughts, and soon took
occasion to ask : "Upon what terms was this pros-
perity promised ?—Terms which Florence has not
fulfilled—repentance for her evil doings. This
must be your first work," and now, as ever before,
repentance was faithfully urged.

Then he reminded them of the quiet revolution ;
of the day they became a free people ; of the exit
of Charles VIII., and urged them to believe his
words now, as then, saying : " Put your trust in
the Lord. I earnestly long to see the whole city
turning to God." Those who trusted him left the
church comforted. The Arrabbiati went out to
invent new schemes for his destruction.

Two days later, word reached Florence that
ships laden with corn, which were believed to have
been lost, had reached Leghorn. Thereat, even
his enemies admitted that Savonarola had this
time proved himself a prophet indeed. The moral
effect of this timely relief, in the cheerfulness of the
people, was most grateful to Savonarola.

The hour of adversity over, the friar returned
to his cloister, soon to be visited with a terrific
blow from Alexander, and attended by such demand upon San Marco as its prior at once determined to resist. He could not, as he wrote, " be
terrified by threats of excommunication to do that
which would be poison and perdition to his own
soul and to those of his brethren. We must resist, if we cannot prevail to have the demand withdrawn. We must do as did St. Paul, who, at
Antioch, withstood Peter face to face, because he
was to be blamed." Thus did the conflict open
with the Pope, and near the end of November,
Savonarola entered the pulpit. Thus closed 1496.
Friends and foes, equally, now believed the man's
death assured and close at hand.

Savonarola now appointed Fra Domenico over
the spiritual affairs of the convent, that he himself
might put forth all his energies toward finishing
his " Triumph of the Cross," believing his time was
short.

A little later the carnival of 1497 drew nigh.
Savonarola determined to celebrate it in a manner
Florence had never witnessed. And to this day
she remembers it. Some others also recall it—not
with approbation, but with astonishment. At that
period, probably no other city excelled Florence
in wealth. It was replete with luxury.

Among the carnival customs was the making of
bonfires on the plaza in the evening of Shrove
Tuesday, and the dancing around them while singing songs. The reader will recall that at the last
carnival, a great reform was affected through the
children. This year Savonarola determined a more
sweeping change should take place. To this end
he enlisted, under the generalship of Fra Domen-

ico, a band of youths, who should traverse the city,
"dressed as angels, and calling from door to door
for whatsoever articles were calculated to minister
to luxury, or worldliness, to be consumed upon
the bonfire."

Many delivered up their possessions, while others
considered these "angels" a most unheavenly order.
However, the amount of trinkets, ornaments,
money, books of bad tendency, pictures, sculptures, and designs accumulated, was marvelous.
An immense scaffolding, pyramidal in form, with
fifteen tiers of shelves arranged around it, was
erected on the plaza chosen for the grand display.
The pyramid was filled with fagots; and the
shelves, with the articles to be destroyed. Many
of them were the works of famous artists and
writers. Bartolommeo and Lorenzo di Credi contributed many of their designs.

Women contributed to the senseless waste,
costly India shawls, expensive perfumes, and other
articles innumerable. Men increased the flames
with chess-boards, cards, card-tables, and instru-
ments of music. Burlamacchi relates that for the
collection, before the torch was applied, a mer-
chant of Venice offered nearly twenty thousand
pounds sterling. But his offer was rejected, and
the man's portrait—placed above the colossal figure intended to personify the carnival—was burned
therewith. "A wild mob danced around the
blazing pile to the music of trumpets.

This example of wild excess was followed by
others yet more humiliating. Savonarola had
condemned most worldly amusements as being
contrary to the mind of God; but dancing, he
thought, might be consecrated to his service.
With this view, he employed a notable poet to

write what he called "Sacred Words," to be sung
to favorite airs while the people danced. On one
occasion, even the friars of San Marco came forth
from their cells and danced with the citizens, forming immense circles by joining hands.

From this hour, even in dissolute Florence, the
tide of popular esteem turned strongly against
Savonarola. His political influence, even, began
to decline. Referring to these scenes of extrava-
gance in conduct, a writer remarks: "How humiliating to see a man of deep learning, full of zeal
for the honor of God and for the good of men, led
by monkish fanaticism to regard as an act of
piety that which was but a burlesque on religion."

In terms of increased severity now, the prior
accused priests and friars of "driving the people,
by the influence of pernicious example, into the
sepulcher of ceremonies." "I tell you," he said,
"this sepulcher must be broken up. It is the will
of Christ that the church should be renovated in
its spirit. What does the church herself say?
Listen, and I will tell you. 'He who has money
may enter and do what he lists.' But what says
the Lord? 'Behold, I will stretch forth my hand
and come upon thee, thou degraded one.'"

Alluding to the expected papal excommunication, he cried: "As for me, I pray thee, O Lord,
that it may come quickly. I know there is one at
Rome daily striving to injure me, but he is not
actuated by zeal for religion, he is sunk in servility
to great lords." Savonarola refers to his old
enemy Mariano Gennezzano, of whose scheming to
extinguish him he was ever aware. "I can tell
you the party at Rome does not do my bidding.
If flattery had been my habit, I had not now been
in Florence." Savonarola, no doubt, here alludes

to the offer of a cardinal's hat, made him about a
year previously. "But, O Lord, such things form
no part of my desires. Thy cross is all I desire.
Cause me to be persecuted. I ask that I may shed
my blood for thee, as thou didst thine for me."
Then, pausing a moment, he added, addressing the
friars, " My sons, cast away all doubt, for we shall
surely have the support of the Lord."

Thus did this devoted, truly worthy, but sometimes very injudicious, servant of the Lord, seek to
fortify himself for the sore conflict upon which he
had entered. Although forbidden to preach either
in public or private, he yet resolved to disobey the
interdict and preach on the coming Ascension-day,
May 4, 1497, and for days previously busied himself with his sermon for the occasion. And preach
he did.

# CHAPTER XVI.

EVERY day now increased the activity of Savonarola's foes. On the evening preceding Ascension-day, some of the more rabid of his opponents, aided by a maker of fireworks, contrived a scheme by which the pulpit of the Duomo and its occupant might be blown to atoms during the service next day. But the diabolical plan was abandoned in consideration of the hundreds of innocent lives that would be sacrificed.

Suspecting some such dire project, Savonarola's friends besought him to abandon his purpose of preaching. With exalted courage he answered: "I cannot, through fear of man, leave the congregation without a sermon on the day upon which the Lord commanded his disciples to go preach his doctrines throughout the world." To such a reply his friends were dumb. They left him to his sermon, while they betook themselves to concerting measures for his protection.

Upon entering the Duomo very early next morning, they found the pulpit spread with an ass' skin, through which fine nails had been driven with points upward, that his hand might be pierced if struck upon them. These were quietly removed, and at the hour for service a strong escort conducted Savonarola to the church. A vast throng crowded the structure. Half the multitude were Arrabbiati. There were present many of the Compagnacci—dissolute aristocrats—in fine attire. In

(116)

striking contrast were the hundreds of Piagnoni, simply clad, appearing like genuine worshipers.

The sermon was unusually impressive, but still neither calculated to allay the fears of those who loved him, nor to diminish the hostility of those who sought his life. First, he uttered a few words on faith, which, as he said, "can do all things, overcome all things, regard with indifference this life, sure of that which is to come," and then boldly, but unwisely, resumed his old style. "The times often foretold are now at hand, when it will appear who is devoted to the Lord. The wicked thought to prevent my preaching to-day. They know that from fear of man, I never failed to do my duty. There is not on earth the man who can say he has seen me so fail. I am quite prepared to lay down my life in the discharge of my duty.

"O Lord! free me from those who call me a seducer. Set my soul free. For my body I have no fear. I call the Lord, the virgin, the angels, the saints, to witness that the things revealed by me have come from God, that I have received them by divine inspiration, in long-protracted vigils, for the good of this people now plotting against me." Then addressing those whom he styled "the good," he declared:—

"Ye are sad when ye ought to rejoice. Tribulations are nigh. There will be a war of excommunications, of swords, of martyrdom. The days of trial are come. It is the will of God that I should be the first to meet them. There are those who say I am no prophet; but they do all they can to fulfill my prophecies. Again I tell you that Italy will be laid waste by barbarous nations, and when they make peace one with another, destruction upon destruction will befall perverse Italy. But do you, ye pious, offer up your prayers. God will help you.

"And now, ye evil-minded," hereat a murmur of disapprobation arose from the audience; but as if he did not notice it, Savonarola cried: "O Lord, be not angry with them; forgive them; convert them; they know not what they do." Then, speaking directly to the disturbers, he continued: "Ye wicked ones, ye think ye are in conflict with the vicar; ye are warring against God. Therefore I fight with you, not from any ill-will I bear toward you, but from the love I bear to the Lord. Why turn ye not to the Lord that there may be peace? 'Friar,' thou wilt say, 'thou oughtest not to be preaching, for the Seignory has forbidden thee'"—a Seignory hostile to him was then in power. "That is not true. I ought to abstain from preaching neither through fear, nor at the command of man. I shall be silent only when I believe my sermons will do harm."

At these words, "a tremendous crash was heard; the doors flew open; the people fled as for their lives. It seemed as if the Duomo, shaken to its foundations, was falling in pieces. Every kind of noise was made. Drums were beaten. Benches were thrown. The confusion was frightful. Several of the Seignory sprang to the pulpit, hoping to capture the author of the tumult, but a blow in the face—an indignity never before offered one of that body—from one of the Piagnoni, defeated the attempt."

Holding aloft the crucifix, Savonarola cried: "Trust in this. Fear nothing." His words were drowned in the tumult. Prostrating himself on his knees, he offered a silent prayer. Then, the uproar having quieted somewhat, he passed down the pulpit stairs. The Piagnoni closed around him, raised their spears, crosses, and swords aloft, and conducted him to San Marco.

In the lovely convent grounds, to those who desired to listen to him, Savonarola concluded the discourse so unceremoniously interrupted at the cathedral. That Ascension-day sermon hastened his doom. The dark days crowded on rapidly. Savonarola cheered his friars by saying : " Be not moved by persecutions. Rejoice rather. Not a drop of blood has yet been shed. The Lord will give faith, virtue, and courage for greater things."

The Seignory now issued a proclamation restricting all friars from preaching, and immediately took steps to secure the banishment of Savonarola. But the Piagnoni intimated to that body that such a measure would not be tolerated. Whereupon the Seignory rested in the certainty that the papal excommunication would soon set matters aright. Meantime Alexander understood the entire situation, and saw that the time was ripe for cutting off " this tool of the devil, this curse of the Florentine people."

Convinced that the storm would soon break upon him, Savonarola addressed a letter to the Pope, lamenting that the Holy Father had never heard him preach, but on the contrary had lent a willing ear to the false accusations of his enemies. He was willing to submit to the church, for he had "never taught any doctrine contrary to that of the Fathers, as his 'Triumph of the Cross' would certify to the whole world."

This letter was penned eighteen days after the Ascension-day sermon. Little did he imagine that the terrible edict of excommunication was at that hour on its way to Florence. The paper consumed a whole month in its journey, and met with rather inhospitable treatment. Messenger after messenger failed to deliver the bull, believing it unsafe to meddle with it. And numerous clergy refused to publish it, "because it had not been intrusted to an apostolic commissioner."

The bull alluded, in the usual mysterious way, to one Girolamo Savonarola, vicar of San Marco. Said His Holiness: "We have with great benignity accepted his excuses, but now command those to whom this bull is sent, to declare—on all festival occasions, in the presence of the people—this same Fra Savonarola to be excommunicated, and that he be so held by everyone, inasmuch as he has not obeyed our apostolic injunction. And everyone is prohibited, under like penalty, from rendering him any assistance; from having any communication with him; or expressing any praise of him, inasmuch as he is excommunicated and suspected of heresy."

The dreaded edict was proclaimed in Florence, June 22, 1497, to a large assembly of clergy, minor friars, monks in white, black, and gray. The ceremony was made as impressive as possible. The bells were solemnly tolled ; tapers were lighted ; the edict was gravely read. Then the lights were extinguished ; there were a few moments of breathless stillness ; there was a slow, cat-like tread of "monkish feet;" the church was left in silence and half light.

We must not forget that this awful document, read amid hush and gloom, accused Savonarola only of *suspected heresy*. Was this Alexander's utmost charge against the man? Does not this prove that political not religious reasons prompted its fulmination? Was there not at Rome all this time a Pietro de Medici, eagerly waiting to be reinstated at Florence? And so long as Savonarola's voice could be raised against him, this could not be.

Savonarola obeyed the mandate, so far as to refrain from preaching. But he wrote a letter to "all

Christians and the beloved of God, against surrep-
titious excommunication," in which he held that
"a Christian will not be guilty of sin, when, in order to avoid an unjust excommunication, he avails
himself of the secular power. It is very right to be
humble and courteous to the Pope; but when the
end is not gained by such humility, *then a coura-
geous liberty must be resorted to.*" These words he
quoted from Gerson.

The boldness of the man in declaring the Pope's
bull unjust, increased by tenfold the anxiety of his
friends, who were more resolute than ever in his
support, while his enemies were more intent upon
his utter removal.

The powerful edict soon began to bear fruit.
The Pope had silenced the only voice which had
preached truth to the people. And in one short
month the profligate days of Lorenzo de Medici
revived. Moreover, in Florence the plague now
prevailed, and was slaying its hundreds. The av-
erage deaths, daily, in the city, were seventy. Now,.
if ever, thought his friends, "the friar's voice is
needed to cheer the sick and dying."

Forbidden to visit as a minister of religion, yet
in his own convent Savonarola relieved and comforted to the utmost those intrusted to his care.
He remained at his post, taking no thought for
himself. Yet he nobly took the precaution to send
away the younger friars and novices, and with them
his own brother, Marco Aurelio. Writing of this
scourge, he said, "Some of the friars die as cheer-
fully as if going to a festival." And again, "Some
number the deaths, daily, at one hundred. One
sees nothing but crucifixes and dead people. We
ourselves, thanks be to God, are well. In these numerous deaths another of Savonarola's predictions
was fulfilled. Florence must have thought of this.

# CHAPTER XVII.

## THE TRIAL OF THE FIVE CONSPIRATORS.

BARELY had the terrible plague abated, and the tide of affairs begun to move again, when Florence was plunged into a sea of tumult and excitement. When Pietro de Medici made a second futile attempt to re-enter Florence, it was more than suspected that certain men of high position in the city were in league with him; but who they were was a mystery. But the secret was thus divulged. There had been banished to Rome, on account of his friendship for the Medici, one Lamberta della Antella. A letter from him promising that if the Seignory would grant him a safe-conduct, he would return to the city and reveal some important facts, was placed by its recipient before that body.

The safe-conduct being delayed a little, the impatient Lamberta passed the border-line of the republic. He was instantly arrested, carried to Florence, put to the torture, and forced to reveal the much he knew. His disclosure made, Florence was transfixed with amazement. Why?—On the list of conspirators brought to light, were the names of five of her noblest, most-trusted citizens! Conspicuous among them was the revered Bernardo del Nero, a man of splendid gifts and lofty position. Letters secured, proved that while he held office as one of Florence's chief magistrates, he was aware of Pietro's schemes to return to the city.

(122)

Being at once arrested, the situation of the five men was perilous in the extreme. The bringing them to trial was an undertaking of vast difficulty. Their high social position and their untarnished character made it quite impossible to believe them to be traitors.

In Florence there was a board of eight, whose duty it was to pass sentence upon prisoners of state. To evade the duty in this sad case, it referred the matter to the Seignory. That body declined the hateful task, but in view of the important interests at stake, allowed the eight the assistance of twelve other influential citizens.

The twenty convicted the prisoners of high treason, whereupon the twelve retired, leaving the others to pass the sentence of death. Shrinking from the enmity sure to fall upon them, they wanted the Seignory to take the responsibility. Firmly that powerful body refused it. Somebody then suggested that the case be referred to the Great Council. To this the counsel for the prisoners strongly demurred, on the plea that State offenders should be tried only by the Seignory. Still the latter refused, but consented that the case might be tried by a new body of two hundred chosen for the purpose. That was a step toward the end.

Finally, the new board was filled. One of the two hundred was Francesco Valori, between whom and the honor of being "the first citizen of Florence" there stood one man—Bernardo del nero. It does not appear that a single man of that assembly was chosen for his fitness for the trying duty. It was composed of several boards of magistracy, and the Seignory decided that each board should consider and vote upon the case separately.

Sentence against the men was the immediate re-

sult.    The counsel for the prisoners was in despair.
It insisted that each member of the assembly should
vote by himself, entreating for it with all their eloquence.    " It hoped that pity, at least for Bernardo
del Nero, aged and venerable; pity for Nicoli Ro-
dolfi, but a trifle his junior; pity for Pucci and Tor-
naboni, both brilliant young orators, to whom Florence always listened with rapturous applause,—it
hoped that pity for such men, and pity even for
Florence, in their loss, would prevail, and that not
one man of the assembly would be found willing to
stain his hands in blood so noble, nor be willing to
be the first to record his vote for death."

Francesco Valori realized the gravity of the
situation, but—Bernardo del Nero once put out of
the way, he would be the first man of Florence—
the temptation was greater than he could bear.    So,
boldly approaching the table around which were
grouped the Senate, he gave his vote for " death "
in tones which rang through the whole assembly.
Most of the two hundred quickly followed his
example, and the fate of the five men seemed sealed.

But their counsel now remembered that a law of
1495 made possible an appeal to the Great Council
for every capital offense.    This appeal the counsel
made, but the populace, from the first hostile to the
accused, cried: " Justice must be done.    The republic is in danger."    Yielding to their clamor, the
Seignory refused permission to appeal.    At this
juncture also came letters from Rome furnishing
new proof of the prisoners' guilt.    Every hope
was now lost.    " Death—without delay "—was
unanimously ordained.

The day being quite spent, the Seignory thought
"to-morrow" would be early enough for the sorrowful deed.    Not such was the opinion of Francesco

Valori. He would not wait until to-morrow to become the first citizen of Florence. Grasping the ballot-box, he dashed it upon the table, exclaiming: "Let justice be done! let justice be done! or there will be trouble here." A moment's silence—and he whose office it was passed the ballot-box to the eight. Five gave their votes for execution, three against it. Not to be thus baffled, Valori arose and soon won the dissenting three to his view, "and one by one they did as he bade them."

In the midst of this wild scene, the five prisoners, barefooted and bound with chains, were by their counsel brought into the assembly in the hope that their presence might awaken sympathy for the ill-fated noblemen. Was that the result? The heart of Florence was stone. In all that assembly of magistracy and councils not one syllable of compassion was heard. Yet many present had enjoyed the kindliest social relations with one or all of the manacled men. They were led back to their cells, and "their heads were struck off at midnight."

For a time the Piagnoni—the party of the republic—gained additional power by this act. Commemorative medals were issued, bearing on one side the image of Savonarola, on the other that of Rome, over which was significantly suspended a hand and dagger.

In that hour, which stirred Florence to her foundations, where was the one man whose voice would have been potent, it was believed, to save at least the life of Bernardo del Nero? He was in the convent of San Marco, "correcting the proof-sheets of his 'Triumph of the Cross.'" Speaking of Bernardo, Savonarola said: "I did not advise his death. I should have been glad had he been sent into exile." And of Tornabuoni he remarked, "I recommended him, though coldly, to the mercy of Valori."

Most singularly, as historians affirm, Savonarola himself secured the passage of that law of 1495, which gave to prisoners of state the right of appeal to the Great Council. Historians also state that his request would have secured that right to the prisoners, for his will was potent with Valori. This latter statement is very doubtful. Savonarola was then an excommunicated man, and at that very crisis efforts were making to have the ban recalled. Under these circumstances, it is extremely uncertain if his services would have been even tolerated. Yet it must ever be lamented that he did not make at least an attempt to save these men. He could have but failed. Clemency at this point might have added stability to the republic. Omission of it certainly hastened its downfall.

# CHAPTER XVIII.

ORE and more incurable grew the dispute between the Pope and Savonarola. During the remaining six months of 1497, the Seignory chosen were of the people's party, and frequently begged their ambassador at Rome "to knock incessantly at the Vatican door, and never cease to entreat His Holiness to revoke the edict of excommunication." Such a step was the last in Alexander's thought; and daily he contrived to secure the obnoxious friar more firmly in his grasp. Meanwhile Savonarola passed most of his time in his cell writing vigorous protests against his illegal excommunication, which, for this reason only, he did not consider himself obliged to obey.

Looking back to that somber day with the resplendent example of Luther lying between ourselves and Savonarola, we can but say that, had he utterly thrown off the yoke of Rome and claimed the right to obey only the Holy Scriptures and his conscience, as did Luther twenty-five years later, he would have been consistent in rejecting the authority and edicts of the Pope. But steadily claiming to be a faithful son of the church, his disobedience, as his historian asserts, "appeared a most serious matter, and inconsistent with the course of a true Christian."

Unable to understand—or to approve—Savon-

arola's course toward the executed Florentines,
several of his disciples now left him. And worse
still, a company of disorderly young men, enraged
at the friar's contradictory course, associated themselves together, with Adolpho Spini, Savonarola's
confessed enemy, at their head, " to concert measures for the removal of the excommunicated friar."
Thus records Guicciardini, adding, " Everyone lived
in fear of these violent, roystering companions."

The bribes and fatherly paragraphs of the Pope
having fai.ed to reduce the contumacious monk to
obedience, Alexander now laid aside all disguises.
On the 18th of October a bull was issued forbid-
d:ng him to preach in San Marco, or elsewhere, because he had declared himself to be a man sent
from God, a claim which ought to be confirmed by
miracle.

The prohibition was expressed in terms so strin-
gent that there seemed to be left to Savonarola no
choice but to obey as gracefully as possible, or to
commit the Pope's bull to the flames, as did the
daring monk of Wittenburg. But the inexplicable
Savonarola did neither. "And from this time,"
says the historian, " Fra Girolamo began to go
down in the world."

Early in November, 1497, the Seignory once
more brought their influence to bear upon the Pope
to have the edict of excommunication removed.
But he was inexorable. Furthermore, realizing the
full effect of the step, His Holiness refused to consider any matter under debate between Florence
and the Roman court, until the prior of San Marco
were delivered into his hands. To this requirement
the Seignory refused assent.

On Christmas-day, after six months of silence, in
bold defiance of the excommunication, Savonarola

performed mass three times in the convent, and administered the sacrament to his brethren and other persons. "After this he conducted a solemn procession of monks and friars through the convent cloisters."

On the 1st of February following, the Seignory gave him permission to resume his Lent sermons in the Duomo. And there, as if urged by an irresistible fate, he once more mounted the pulpit stairs, and preached a discourse more than ever denunciatory of the sins of the clergy, and of Alexander himself. The church was filled to overflowing, regardless of the edict of the Archbishop of Florence, forbidding all persons to attend the service, and admonishing the parish priests to watch, lest their flocks should stray away to this son of perdition, and thus cut themselves off from the church, from confession, the sacrament, and burial in consecrated ground.

Entering at once upon the topics uppermost in his mind,—excommunication, the authority of the great pontiff, and freedom of conscience,—Savonarola used language little expected from an obedient son of the church, and which startles us, even at this distance down the stream of time. Hear his astounding sentences, referring to the Pope:—

"When the one appointed by God severs himself from God, he is a broken tool, and is no longer entitled to our obedience! Our perfection consists not in faith, nor in law, but in charity, and he alone who has this knows what is needful to salvation. Whoever, therefore, commands anything contrary to charity, which is the fullness of the law, let him be anathema! Were it an angel even who said it, were all the saints, and the Virgin Mary—which certainly is not possible—to say so, let them be

9

anathematized! And if any Pope has ever spoken
in contradiction to what I am now saying, let him be
excommunicated!

"Some among you are afraid that, although this
edict is null in the sight of God, it may be valid in
the eye of the church. For me *it is sufficient that I
am not bound by it, but by Christ.* Shall I tell you
how absolution is to be obtained? Ah, it were better for me to be silent. Yet this much will I say:
This is the way." Then, taking two keys, he struck
them together to imitate the clinking of money,
thereby implying that absolution could be pur-
chased with money, in the church in that day.
The Catholic Church never changes.

Is it any wonder that Alexander grew restless
with such doctrines thundered forth by one he had
excommunicated. He dreaded what else might be
said by this man, dead to fear, callous to favor.
Shortly after this scene in the Duomo, Savonarola
discoursed in San Marco on the duties and character of the priesthood, finishing with a few sentences
never more applicable than to-day.

"O my brethren! when I think of the life led by
priests, I cannot refrain from tears. I pray you
weep over their vices, that the Lord may, for the
sake of his church, bring the priests to repentance;
for all must see that a great scourge is hanging
over them. In Rome they make a mockery of
Christ and of the saints; they are worse than the
Turks and the Moors. They even make a traffic
of the sacraments. Do you think that Jesus Christ
will endure this? Woe, woe to Italy and to Rome!
Come forth, come forth from the midst of her, ye
priests. Let us see, my brethren, whether we cannot in some degree revive the word of God."

Then, addressing the Divine One, he exclaimed:

"O Father! we shall be put to death; we shall be sent to prison; we shall be persecuted and put to death. Be it so; let them do as they will; they cannot tear Christ from my heart; my desire is to die for my God."

Savonarola preached also on Sexagesima Sunday that year, 1498, and gave utterance to these ringing opinions on the doctrine of papal infallibility: "I take it for granted that there is no man who is not liable to err. We have had many Popes who have gone astray. If it were true that the Pope can do no wrong, we need but follow his example to be saved. You will say, perhaps, that as a man the Pope can do wrong, but not in his capacity as Pope. I reply, The Pope may err in his ecclesiastical censures and judgments. How many have been the laws made by one Pope and annulled by another! How many opinions held by one have been repudiated by another!"

The carnival of 1498 was a very different affair from its predecessor. There was a vast destruction of "vanities" by fire, on the plaza, it is true. But the Compagnacci, and others equally tender of heavenly things, handled the "angels," sent around to collect the articles, with very little mercy. On the top of the very miscellaneous pile was placed a gigantic figure of Lucifer, encircled by representations of the seven mortal sins—as taught by the Catholic Church. As the match touched the great heap, the crowd gathered around and profanely sang the Te Deum, while the smoke and flames and bits of burning property rose high in the air.

As in the previous year, the alms collected were carried to the charitable institutions for which they were intended. Then a procession of monks, friars, and citizens marched to San Marco, planted a cru-

cifix, and around the should-be-sacred symbol
danced in a delirium of excitement, chanting psalms
and hymns. With such scenes ended the carnival
of 1498, in elegant and cultured Florence, in cruel
and heathenish Florence; Florence, wherein at that
hour the tide of the "new learning" was at its
flood. Long were the consequences of those deeds
remembered by both the friends and foes of Savonarola.

Indeed, his late sermons, and the scenes which
took place at that carnival, doubled the fury of his
enemies. Rome was crazed with anger, as reports
of his Lent sermons, and of these carnival festivities,
reached her ears. And more furious than ever was
Savonarola against Rome. Immediately the Pope
sent out an edict, declaring he would make "that
worm of a preaching friar feel the full weight of his
wrath." Notwithstanding, every one of these sermons were printed, and greedily read by the people
in Florence, in all Italy, beyond the Alps.

Strozzi wrote from Rome: "They begin to hear
something of the new preaching in this city, and I
doubt not we shall come to blows." And Bonsi,
the Florentine ambassador at Rome, sent this word
to Savonarola: "I am beset by a multitude of cardinals and prelates, all of whom blame the Seignory,
and declare that the Pope's rage is terrific. You
have many enemies here who are blowing the fire."

Savonarola well knew who was chief among the
fire-fanners at Rome. The vindictive Gennezzano
had ever promised to make his rival in oratory feel
the weight of his hand. So important now did the
accusing priest's charges against Savonarola appear
to Alexander, that he requested him to present
them from the pulpit. With most unseemly read-
iness he consented. But so personal and unworthy

was his address that his hearers turned away in
disgust. And the many prelates who looked for
information of importance, shook their heads in
displeasure.

Into the Pope's hands at this crisis fell one
of Savonarola's recent sermons on the Exodus.
Forthwith there went out of Rome a command to
the Seignory, closing in these suggestive terms : "If
you refuse obedience to this order, then, in order
that the dignity and authority of the Holy See may
be maintained, we shall be forced to pass an interdict upon your city, and to have recourse to other
measures still more effective." Thus threatened
the great " Head of the Church." Fearful had the
storm become, but Savonarola bent not before it,
and went on preaching in San Marco.

There had been in office, now, three successive
Seignories that were favorable to the prior. But
early in March a new board was elected, with but
three of its nine members friendly to him. Encouraged by this change, Alexander repeated his
demand to have the monk sent to Rome. To his
astonishment, the Seignory refused, not from at-
tachment to the friar, nor his teachings, but because
he was a Florentine citizen. To suffer him to be
tried by any foreign authority, would be a stain
upon the independence of the commonwealth.

This attitude of resistance was not assumed by
the Seignory single-handed. Too much it dreaded
the odium inseparable from the position ; so, to
support the weak body, an assembly of magistrates
was convened. Several of the latter had been much
tried with Savonarola's obstinacy, and, moreover,
possessed a fervent zeal " for the honor of God," or
for—what was the same thing to them—" obedience
to the Pope." But these conscientious men were

happily in the minority.    To the members generally, the honor of the commonwealth was quite as
precious as was obedience to Alexander.    So, with
surprising shrewdness, it was suggested that if Savonarola's preaching were restricted to San Marco,
"God and the commonwealth would be properly
honored," and the Pope's dignity duly respected.

The delicate matter thus adjusted, Savonarola
preached regularly at the convent.    But what said
the Pope?    Brief followed brief, expressing his dis-
satisfaction.    He marveled " how the Seignory could
have so far forgotten the respect due to both him
and themselves as to aid and abet the contemptible
reptile."    Every letter contained an order for the
monk to appear at Rome to answer charges, and
purge himself of his contumacy.    " The mercy
of the Mother Church would be vouchsafed should
he recant ; but if not, the Holy Father would resort
to extreme measures against him.    And, further,
were he not obeyed, he would confiscate all property in Rome belonging to Florentine citizens, and
also forbid his subjects to have any dealings with
the commonwealth ;    and, further still, he would
impose the same restrictions on other nations, on
pain of interdict!"

Did the Seignory send the friar to Rome?    They
simply forbade his preaching in San Marco.    Whereupon the baffled Pope wrote that body a letter expressing his "joyful contentment," wisely conclud-
ing, no doubt, that the stubborn Florentines would
concede no more.    The Seignory was careful to re-
late to him, however, the wonderful spiritual effects
of Savonarola's sermons.

Before the order of the magistrates imposing
total silence reached Savonarola, he preached a
most tender sermon, exclusively to the women of

his charge, as had been his custom once a week for
some time.   Sorrowful in tone, its effect was very
great.   Many of the noblest women of Florence
were in the audience.   At one stage, he exclaimed:
"O Lord, we ask not tranquility from thee; not
that tribulation shall cease, but we do ask for the
Spirit; we ask for thy love.   Grant unto us gratitude
and grace to overcome adversity.   We would that
thy love should bless the earth."

The anticipated restriction reached him that
evening.   To the bearer Savonarola said, "You
come, I presume, from your masters."   "From
their Lordships, the Seignory, certainly," he replied.   The friar rejoined, "I also must consult
*my* Lord.   To-morrow you shall receive my
answer."

The "to-morrow," March 18, 1498, heard his
last sermon.   He informed his audience of the prohibition he had received, and expressed his purpose
to obey it.   He said: "These are evil tidings for
Florence.   Misfortunes are about to fall on her.
You fear the papal interdict, but the Lord will
send an interdict by which the wicked shall lose
both goods and life. . . .   When the whole
ecclesiastical power is corrupt, you must turn to
Christ, who is the First Cause, and say, 'Thou art
my Confessor, Bishop, and Pope.'"

After this, Savonarola gave two or three ad-
dresses, but they could hardly be termed sermons.
For eight consecutive years, now, as he himself
states—and as he predicted at his coming—he had
preached in giddy Florence, with but several short
absences.   And during that period he was *the one*
distinguished preacher of the age.   During the Advent and Lent seasons of all those years he had
not failed to preach daily.   During the intervals he
preached on all festival days.

Savonarola lived in one of the most corrupt eras of all human history ; he preached when the professed church of God was sunk in a night of iniquity. With all his strength he preached repentance of sin, and faith in the Lord Jesus Christ as a Saviour from sin, and as the only ground of hope for fallen man. He preached righteousness with almost superhuman energy. He preached charity, the highest quality in the Christian religion. Yet his life appears to have been but a partial success, except in its distant results. What was the matter?

A very few sentences will sum up the causes of the great man's failure, if we may call it a failure. First, he clung with amazing tenacity to the corrupt church which he so mercilessly denounced, his example and preaching thus losing half their power. He seemed not to perceive that the teachings of Rome are antagonistic to the gospel of Christ; thus were his views of that gospel defective. Second, when at the zenith of his influence for good, he unwisely mingled service to the republic with service to God.

Had Savonarola but broken utterly away from the corrupt church, had he but left the republic to build its own fabric, had he but labored to make Florence free through the truth only, his life might have been crowned, not only with the martyrdom he craved, but with a nobler success. But the light was midnight in his day. He stood alone, too. The wonder with regard to him is the influence he exerts, to-day, over the race. But the end draws near.

# CHAPTER XIX.

## THE ORDEAL BY FIRE.

S Savonarola's sky grew darker, many of his followers deserted him. Some fled from the city. Others concealed themselves until the storm, about to break, had passed. Just at this juncture of affairs, there occurred within Florence itself an event which involved Savonarola in rank fanaticism, and hastened his end. The Franciscan order of friars, long jealous of the great Dominican, and instigated by the Arrabbiati, determined his ruin. Francesco de Puglia—a Franciscan—had himself long condemned Savonarola's teachings from the pulpit. Of this no notice was taken. Being called a heretic, a schismatic, a pretended prophet, had no effect upon the prior. So Francesco, at no loss for expedients, challenged Savonarola to prove his doctrines by the ordeal by fire—passing between lines of burning fagots.

Savonarola treated the proposal with deserved contempt. But, unfortunately, his too zealous friend and disciple, Fra Domenico, present once when the challenge was given, eagerly accepted it. Unhappily, however, Savonarola had announced that on the first day of the carnival he would go forth with any one of his adversaries, sacrament in hand, and solemnly call upon God to send down fire from heaven to consume whichever one was in error. The day arrived. Savonarola left San Marco, and ascended the pulpit of the cathedral, filled with thousands anxious to witness the miracle.

First came the sermon, without a particle of his old fiery eloquence. Then, leaning over the pulpit, he said : " Citizens of Florence, if in the name of God I have said to you anything which was not true ; if the apostolic edict is valid ; if I have deceived anyone, pray God that he will send down fire and consume me, in the presence of the people. And *I* pray God, Three in One, whose body I hold in this blessed sacrament, to send death to me in this place, if I have not preached the truth."

For a half hour the audience prayed and waited for fire from heaven. It came not. Savonarola and his brethren returned to the convent chanting a Te Deum. Shortly after that, Savonarola foolishly challenged the Franciscans to accompany him to a neighboring cemetery and there to raise the dead. The proposal was declined, but it probably led the Franciscans again to demand the ordeal by fire. Again the prior firmly opposed the step.

But Domenico, having accepted the challenge, was the last man to repent. On the other hand, when Francesco saw that Domenico really held himself ready to brave the fire, he was the more anxious to escape. He attempted this, by declaring he would enter the fire only with Savonarola. " Surely," thought the Franciscan, " Fra Girolamo has too much sense to enter the burning pile ; I need not now fear ; and as for Domenico, he is but an ardent fanatic, ready to sacrifice life in Savonarola's cause." Savonarola resolutely declined. Then Francesco, impelled by the Compagnacci— the band of dissolute young men already mentioned —who had taken up the matter, induced a brother monk, Guiliamo Rondinelli, to take his place in the ordeal, with Fra Domenico. Rondinelli assented, saying " he should be burned, but he ventured his life for the salvation of souls."

Day after day was fixed upon for the ordeal, and then set aside. The Pope was eager for it. For their own ends the Seignory desired it. The Piagnoni loudly demanded it, having not a doubt but that Savonarola would lead the way, followed by the loyal Domenico, and of course they would come forth with not even the smell of fire on their garments.

Finally the disappointed people called loudly for the spectacle. The trial was set for the 7th of April. That morning, the plaza was early occupied by three bodies of armed men—" five hundred soldiers in the pay of the Seignory; five hundred ruffians under Dolpho Spini, leader of the Compagnacci; and three hundred Piagnoni, led by Marucceo Salviati."

While these movements were taking place on the plaza, Savonarola performed mass at the convent, and addressed the people assembled. Then the mace-bearers of the Seignory arrived, saying all was ready. Four hundred Dominicans then marched forth, led by Fra Domenico. " He wore a bright-colored cope, and in his hand carried a long cross. Behind him walked Savonarola, robed in white, bearing the host in a crystal vase." All chanted, " Let God arise; let his enemies be scattered." At noon the Dominicans reached the plaza. Since before dawn every inch of space had been occupied.

In full view of the vast assembly of armed men and citizens rose the huge pile of material prepared for this outrage upon common sense and humanity. First, there was a platform about eighty feet long by ten feet wide, paved with brick and elevated about four feet from the ground. On this platform were heaped masses of fagots, saturated with oil. Between these heaps was left a space about two feet wide the entire length of the platform. Here the

champions of faith were to walk, amid the leaping
flames.  They were to enter at the end nearest the
palace.  As soon as they had entered, that end was
to be immediately closed by lighted fagots so that
neither could turn back.  This precaution was the
suggestion—of Savonarola!  But why should he
think the men might retreat?  Did he not expect
God to protect them from the fire?

Now everything seems to be ready.  The weary
crowd is impatient.  Fra Domenico is praying before the altar upon which Savonarola laid the host.
The low and solemn chanting of the Dominicans
comforts him.  But where are Francesco de Puglia
and Rondinelli?—Holding a secret conference with
the Seignory in the palace.  Now Domenico rises
from prayer, his face calm in the conviction that
God will sustain him.  He begs earnestly that there
be no more delay.  Then Savonarola steps forward
and demands that the Franciscan come forth.
There is no reply, no movement.  Now members
of that order near began to object to Domenico's
dress, first one article then another, until a complete change had been effected, on the plea that
" Savonarola might have cast some spell upon them
to prevent their burning."  Finally, they forbade
Domenico to stand near the prior.  So Domenico
placed himself among the objectors themselves.

Now there is a slight agitation of the crowd near
the palace entrance.  All is expectation for a moment.  Then the old quiet is resumed.  No Rondinelli appears.  On all sides fierce threats now rend
the air.  The Franciscan champion has asked another conference with the Seignory.  This known,
the Arrabbiati improve the opportunity, spring from
their ranks, and try to seize Savonarola.  Instantly,
Salviati, at the head of the three hundred Piagnoni

drawn up in the front of the Dominicans, draws
a line on the ground with his sword, exclaiming:
" The man who crosses that line, shall try the metal
of Muruccio Salviati's arms." Back drew the Arrabbiati. The populace resumed its waiting. Sa-
onarola anxiously inquired the cause of the delay.

A heavy thunder-shower, which had gathered
suddenly, now drenched the crowd, giving hope to
the nobler Florentines that a stop might thus be
put to the scandalous proceedings. But the sun
soon reappeared, warm and bright as before. Still
no Rondinelli. His friends, to excuse his absence,
now demanded that Domenico should lay aside the
crucifix. At once he assented, saying he would
hold the host in his hand. This provoked some
discussion, and at that moment the Seignory announced that " the ordeal by fire would not proceed."

Many of the multitude had not tasted food since
the dawn, and their fury now became frightful.
Every party and faction was extremely disappointed,
even enraged, over being "cheated of the miracle."

Upon Savonarola alone fell the furious storm of
accusations. Even the Piagnoni admitted that he
had proved himself an unreliable leader. When
others refused, said they, he ought resolutely to
have walked into the fire, and thus proved his divine mission. The Seignory, who had put a stop
to the proceedings, declared the disappointment
was due to the cowardice of Savonarola, and proclaimed him a deceiver of the people. And the
audacious Franciscans claimed the victory!

Defended by a faithful few, Savonarola returned
to San Marco, amid a raging crowd hurling upon
him every contemptuous epithet. When once the
walls of his cell closed around him that night, what
must have been his thoughts!

# CHAPTER XX.

## THE FATAL PALM SUNDAY.

PALM SUNDAY was the day after the forbidden ordeal. Disregarding the command of the Seignory not to preach even in San Marco, Savonarola addressed a company whose faith in him was unswerving. The sermon ended, in tones of deepest sadness he pronounced the benediction, and slowly descended the pulpit steps, nevermore to enter that chapel. This act of disobedience indicates that he felt his time was short, and he would improve it to the utmost. Alluding to this act, Nardi, the historian, says, "This man was ever true to himself; he was never intimidated by any trouble or danger."

After vespers at the convent, a company of Piagnoni proceeded to the Duomo, where Fra Mariano, the Dominican, who also had offered to pass through the fire, was appointed to preach. The church was packed. The Compagnacci crowded the nave. At the doors were stationed the Arrabbiati, to assure those entering that no sermon would be given. This the Piagnoni firmly denied. The Arrabbiati replied with a shower of stones. Instantly swords were drawn, and forthwith a mob was instituted. Those of the audience who had come unarmed, rushed out for their weapons. From the plaza was heard the cry, "The fire to San Marco!"

Barely were the words uttered, when church and convent were besieged by the infuriated throng. A few women were at prayers in the chapel. They now fled, shrieking, driven by a discharge of stones. Several faithful friends of Savonarola remained in the church, and barred its doors, and also those of the convent, determining to defend the sacred ground. They had clearly foreseen this storm, and, without Savonarola's knowledge, had brought into the convent pikes, muskets, and other fire-arms. These were distributed among the lay brethren, and a few frairs, also armed, joined the ranks.

Savonarola was much displeased, and the saintly Domenico prayed them not to stain their hands with blood, so opposed both to the gospel and Savonarola's teachings. And truly the sight of a Dominican accoutered with helmet and halberd was unutterably offensive to the prior. Putting on his cope and taking the crucifix, he entreated his brethren to let him surrender, and thus prevent shedding of blood. "Let me go, for I know this tempest has arisen on my account," he prayed. But they gathered about him, saying, "If you go, you will be torn in pieces, and then what shall we do?"

Their words prevailed. Turning, Savonarola said, "Follow me," and together they passed through the cloisters singing a joyful hymn. It was now about four in the afternoon. A vast multitude filled the plaza. Taking position in front of the people, the mace-bearers of the Seignory made an announcement from that body. Of course it was a command to the rioters to disperse! Far from it. This it was: "All *within the convent* are commanded to lay down arms. All laymen are to depart from it. Savonarola is to quit Florentine territory within twelve hours!" A tumultuous cry from the mob was the only answer.

As night closed in, the friars, faint and weary, ate a few figs to refresh themselves. The shots now became more frequent, the cries more fearful. All through the night, into the morning, the invaders had their will. They scaled the convent walls, broke in its windows, set fire to its doors, and through the flames effected an entrance. Immediately the entire structure was in possession of the mob. Even the infirmary, and the cells where were men praying, were invaded. Springing to their feet, the terrified monks fought until their assailants turned away. The next moment, meeting another band of plunderers, the friars entered the choir. Then began the great bell of the convent to toll, amid the din of arms and cries of foes.

During those long hours, on his knees in the choir, Savonarola entreated the Lord for himself, his brethren, the church, and the convent. At one time, upon the steps of the high altar, close beside him, was laid a young man mortally wounded. Fra Domenico administered to him the Lord's Supper just before he died in his arms. Soon thick smoke forced them to break the windows for air.

Then Savonarola rose from his knees, and bade those present to follow him to the library. Taking position in the center of its great hall, Savonarola spoke his last words to his brethren:—

" My sons, before God and in the presence of the holy sacrament, our enemies being already in possession of the convent, I confirm to you my teaching. All that I have said to you I have received from God. He is my witness in heaven that I have spoken the truth. I did not know that all Florence would thus turn against me. But God's will be done. Have faith, patience, and prayer. Let these be your arms. I leave you with sorrow and anguish, to go into the hands of the enemy. I know not if they will take my life. Be of good courage."

Scarcely had he spoken when a body of guards

arrived from the Seignory, ordering the convent to be reduced by artillery unless Fra Girolamo Savonarola, Fra Domenico, and Fra Salvestro were immediately delivered into the hands of the Seignory. Request was sent also for the presence of Francesco Valori, who, with other leading Piagnoni, was at the convent devising means for the safety of Savonarola. Valori obeyed reluctantly, but with the hope, it is said, of rallying all the Piagnoni to the rescue.

But on the way to the palazzo, he was recognized by relatives of Ridolfi and Tornabuoni, the two young Florentine conspirators, whose deaths he had procured the previous August. Instantly he was cut down near his own palace. Hearing the noise in the street, his wife ran to a window to learn the cause, and was killed without a word of warning. Their home was then sacked by the mob.

Further resistance seeming futile, Savonarola confessed to Domenico, and from his hands received the sacrament, and Salvestro not being found, Savonarola and the faithful Domenico, though urged to escape at the rear of the convent, as Valori had done, scorned the entreaty, and left the convent, surrounded by the murderous mob. As he turned to go, Savonarola, embracing each friar, said to them: " My brethren, remember never to doubt. The work of the Lord is ever progressive. My death will serve but to hasten it." Betrayed by the monk Maletesta, who only two days before had offered to accompany Domenico through the fire, Salvestro was soon dragged forth, and the three prisoners, pressed forward by the ferocious crowd, soon gained the palazzo publico, with their faces blackened by smoke from torches thrust under their hoods, while the bearers insultingly cried, " This is the new light."

The prisoners were hurried into the presence of the chief magistrate, who inquired if they still maintained that the doctrines they had preached were from God. Replying in the affirmative, they were hurried to their cells. Savonarola's prison was the chamber in the tower of the palazzo, of which Cosmo de Medici had once been the occupant.

Without delay the various European courts were notified of Savonarola's arrest. The Florentine ambassador at Rome was charged to ask absolution of Alexander for the sin of the Seignory in so long permitting Savonarola to preach. Alexander's response abounded in commendation of these "true sons of the church;" freely granted them absolution; promised them every blessing, present or future; commanded them to hasten the trial of Savonarola for his state offenses, and then to speed him to Rome to answer for his disobedience to the Holy Father.

We close this chapter by adding that on the 7th of April, the day set for the ordeal by fire, Charles VIII., of France, died, miserably, at Amboise. Suddenly stricken with apoplexy, he was borne into a hut near by, where he expired upon a bed of mere straw. The king's death was a heavy blow to the political structure Savonarola had reared. He was its last and most powerful support. Often had the friar prophesied that, should Charles not fulfill his duty in chastising Italy and reforming the church, God would forsake him and he would die wretchedly. The exact fulfillment of these predictions did not seem to impress the Seignory with the conviction that the mission of the man they were about to put to death might, after all, be from God.

# CHAPTER XXI

## TRIAL OF SAVONAROLA.

SO eager was the Seignory to engage in the trial of Savonarola and his brethren that, on the evening after the riot, that board held a meeting for their examination. That day was Monday in Easter week, a week which Savonarola had been accustomed to consecrate with special services in the Duomo. But now the multitude, which had listened, enraptured, to his fervid eloquence, shouted for his death. Besides Domenico and Salvestro, seventeen others of his tried friends were in the hands of his determined enemies.

Having searched San Marco, and particularly Savonarola's cell, for evidence against him, the Compagnacci collected all the weapons they could find at the convent, placed them, stained with blood, upon a vehicle, and paraded them through the streets, crying, "See the miracles of the friar, the tokens of his love for Florence!" The sight was shocking, and had the desired effect, that of paving the way for the merciless deeds to come.

Instead of the regular Council of Eight, a special commission of seventeen, all open enemies of Savonarola, was appointed to conduct the trial, with authority to employ torture or other means deemed necessary to gain their end. Of this cruel court, Dolfo Spini, leader of the unprincipled Compagnacci, sat as judge. Openly and secretly, by his own hand and by that of an assassin, had this man

(147)

sought to kill Savonarola. So shocked was one of the Seignory at all this pretense at justice, in which he was expected to act a part, that he withdrew from the board, exclaiming, " God forbid that my family should stain its hands with the blood of this just man! "

The commission was formally made up May 14. But in such haste were his foes to begin their work that Savonarola was examined by torture on the evening of the 9th, and for ten days following. Questioned as to his doctrine, he replied, " You tempt the Lord." And when requested to give his opinions in writing, his statements were so direct, so clear, so free from views which could be urged against him, that the document was instantly torn in pieces. This was the only formulation of his faith made during the trial, and is forever lost.

At length, tortured beyond endurance, in an agony of pain, weakened by months of sleeplessness and of intense mental strain, he admitted, again and again, all they wished. But the moment torture was removed, he recalled what he had said in the frenzy of suffering.

On one occasion, conscious of his mental weakness, he cried out, "Take, O Lord! take, oh, take my life away!" But instead of death came delirium. Thus succeeded ten days of torture and mental overthrow. Yet his "examiners" affirmed that his answers, given when in that condition, were rendered "spontaneously, in an uninjured state of the body!" After one of these examinations, as they were about to send him to his cell, he fell upon his knees and prayed for his tormentors.

At no time of his life had Savonarola been able to explain to others the subject of his visions. It was impossible that now, with his body in agony from torture, he could render a clear opinion in regard to them. In such moments he felt his weakness, and at one time exclaimed, " O Lord! thou hast taken from me the spirit of prophecy." At another, firmly adhering to all he had uttered respecting his visions, he used these remarkable words:—

" Leave this subject alone; for if it be from God, you will have a clear sign of it; but if it be of man, it will fall to the ground. *But whether I am a prophet or not, is not an affair of the State; and no one has a right to condemn the thoughts of others.*"

Savonarola's answers in reference to political matters were clear and unequivocal. Again and again he denied having used the confessional to obtain a knowledge of state secrets. " My sole object has ever been to favor free government in general, and such laws as would improve it," he once said.

Torture daily repeated, torture so severe as to make even the one who applied it stand aghast at its effects, failed to elicit anything which could legally condemn Savonarola, and the case now seemed desperate. The people were impatient for his conviction. The Pope wondered at the prolonged trial. What should the Seignory do? This they did. After a long day of unsuccessful torture and questioning, one of the examiners met upon the street a notary of infamous character, named Seccone, and bewailed the fact that no degree of painful torture had drawn from Savonarola a particle of legal evidence against him.

"Then," answered the notary, " where none exists we must invent one. I will undertake to make out a process that will convict him," and offered to do the despicable work " for four hundred ducats." The proposition was accepted. He was concealed in the room for torture, and there from the mass of incoherent utterances of the agonized victim, Seccone drew up an acute and strong document, which, though by no means satisfactory to the Seignory, was accepted, and, with numerous revisions, was published by it. Still, not even the shrewdness of the unprincipled Seccone procured sentence of death against the prisoner. So the Seignory turned the lawyer off with but thirty ducats.

This document, circulated in Florence, was read with astonishment. Friend nor foe of Savonarola believed it to be genuine. "The first copy had barely been sold when the Seignory suppressed the entire edition." It was believed this step would relieve the board of the odium which must inevitably attach to the party, whether Pope or Seignory, which secured the conviction of the prisoner. Of this act of suppression, the historian, Burlamacchi, remarks: "God permitted the document to be divulged; for Seccone had sent it to a friend, who promised not to show it to anyone, but he deceived him, printed it, and so made it public."

Once more Savonarola was subjected to "examination," short and frightfully severe. Once more tormentors made his words mean just what they willed. The law required the report of the trial to be read in the hall of the Great Council, before the public, in the presence of the accused. But there Savonarola would instantly discover its falsehoods, and that would not do. So it was read in his absence, by the secretary of the Council of Eight, who audaciously assured the throng that "Savonarola declined to be present lest he should be stoned!" Not a soul present believed the statement.

From the 19th of April to the 19th of May, Savonarola lived quietly in his prison, free from examination by torture. On the latter date, since the Seignory had been unable to find a legal verdict of

death against him, and since the matter of his condemnation had been referred to the Pope, the two
papal commissioners, the bishops Romolino and
Turriano, arrived in Florence, with orders from the
Pope to secure the friar's death, "though he were a
second John the Baptist."

In his cell, during that month of repose, his frail
and broken body having recovered a little, Savonarola found pure solace in writing out his medita-
tions upon the thirty-first and fifty-first psalms.
Hear these touching lines from his reflections upon
the latter: "Now let the world oppress me as it
will. Let mine enemies rise up against me. As
one whose hope is in the Lord, I fear them not. It
may be, O Lord, that thou wilt not grant that I
may be delivered from temporal anguish, for such
measure of grace might not help the soul. Virtue
alone inspires it with courage in days of tribulation.
For a time, then, I shall be overcome by men.
They will have power against me. But thou wilt
not suffer that I shall be forever cast down.

" I shall erelong be freed from tribulation. And
by what merits ? Truly not by mine own, but by
thine, O Lord. I do not rely upon mine own justification, but on thy mercy. Justification comes
from grace alone; no one will be justified before
God solely by having fulfilled the works of the law.
I shall not put my trust in man, but in the Lord
alone. For the death of saints is precious in the
eyes of the Lord. Should the whole army of mine
enemies be arrayed against me, my heart will not
quake. Thou art my refuge, and wilt lead me to
my latter end."

"Savonarola was then deprived of pen and ink,
and could write no more."

# CHAPTER XXII.

## DOMENICO AND SALVESTRO.

ESS satisfactory, if possible, proved the examination of Domenico and Salvestro. Mentally and physically robust, Domenico endured the torture triumphantly. Not a word could the examiners extort from him to the detriment of Savonarola. Too long and familiarly had he known his beloved leader to now believe him untrue. As with Savonarola, so now they desired Domenico to state in writing his confession of faith, that it might be published. He complied; and so true, so excellent, was every sentence, that the document told only against themselves. Publish it they dared not. So they mangled and changed it and his confessions, until they made them betray friends of Savonarola, a thing to which death would have been preferable to Fra Domenico. But even then the public must not see it. A few manuscript copies, only, were privately circulated.

The statement began: "My God and Lord, Jesus Christ, knows that I, Fra Domenico, for his sake, am not false in anything I now write." Then he proceeded to say that both he and Savonarola were free from the blood shed in San Marco. The arms were brought in and concealed there without their knowledge. Referring to the ordeal by fire, he affirmed: "I went forth with the utmost deliberation to pass through the fire, never expecting an objection would be raised to my carrying the host. I beg that my words may be interpreted according to the intention with which they are written."

Domenico was requested to state in writing his opinion of Savonarola. His assent was instant. He wrote: " I have ever fixedly believed, and nothing has ever caused me to disbelieve, and I do now believe, in the prophecies of Savonarola. I have steadfastly kept to that faith. Nor ought your excellencies to be offended on that account, *for this belief does no injury to the state. In such matters everyone is free to believe as he will."* Now follow words so genuine, so affecting, that even at this distant day one cannot read them without a feeling of agony that such men, or any man, should ever have died for opinion's sake.

" There is nothing more on my mind. If you wish to ask me anything else, I will do my best to satisfy you. But give credit to all I say, for I have ever had a tender conscience. I am quite ready to speak as if at the point of death, which may very easily be the case, if you continue to torture me, for I am already utterly broken down. I pray you be merciful and believe in the simple truth I have written." Unrelenting, they proceeded with the torture, until in his misery, he cried :—

" I know no more. My whole concern has been to lead a life of virtue, and with Jesus Christ as king of Florence. You can get nothing more out of me. I have nothing more to give." Unmoved, they continued the torture. When suffering almost unto death, they placed a pen in his hand and he heroically wrote: "God's will be done! I never perceived nor had the slightest suspicion that Father Hieronymo either deceived or feigned. On the contrary, he was ever most upright. He was a man of rare nature. I have sometimes said to the friars, that if I ever discovered in him the slightest error or deception, I would make it public. It is most certain I have sometimes declared this to himself. And this I would now do, did I know there is duplicity in him."

To all this stout-heartedness of Domenico, Salvestro's weakness presented the greatest contrast. To save his life he was willing to utter and then retract anything; to swear falsely against Savonarola; to disclose the names of his friends. Nevertheless, some of his confessions established beyond doubt Savonarola's innocence. For this reason his deposition was placed in Seccone's hands for revision, and for *additions* if need be.

The monks were led back to their cells. Then proceeded the examination of the others under arrest. Without an exception, all declared the friar to be "a man wholly devoted to heavenly things." But when confronted with Seccone's report of Savonarola's denial of his visions and prophecies, the surprise and indignation of some knew no bounds.

Soon after Savonarola's arrest, two friars of San Marco were dispatched to Rome with a letter imploring Alexander's pardon for having harbored "*that fomenter and leader in every error!*" Yet, most inconsistently, the letter affirms that "the rectitude of Savonarola's life, the sanctity of his habits, the success which attended his efforts to reclaim Florence from vice, usury, and every crime, had deceived not only themselves, but men of far greater genius." Readily the Pope absolved these cowardly men. He also addressed to the Florentine archbishop, and to the Chapter of the Duomo, a letter authorizing them " to grant absolution for any crime against Savonarola, even were it that of murder." In both letters he demanded that Savonarola should receive sentence of death at Rome.

# CHAPTER XXIII.

## SAVONAROLA AND HIS FRIENDS DIE.

HE two papal commissioners were Turriano, General of the Dominican Order, and Francesco Romolino, Bishop of Ilerda. As the bishops entered Florence on the 19th of May, all around them rang the cry: " Let him die!" "Death to the friar!" Romolino, surveying the crowd, smiled and replied, " Yes, he will die, sure enough." Barely had the commissioners entered the apartment assigned to them, when, turning to the magistrates present, Romolino said: " We shall make a famous blaze! I have the sentence already!"

The following day these zealous men began the investigation. Torture was the initial step. These papal messengers exceeded even the Seignory in cruelty. The same result was attained—the same steady denial of false teaching, of political crimes— the same incoherent answers, and, finally, loss of reason. Thus passed two days, the bishops learning that neither by torment of body, cross-questioning, nor distortion of language, could they fix upon one point that would legally convict him. True, he sometimes promised to recant, but the moment torture ceased, he reaffirmed his innocence. Once he cried out: " My God, I denied thee for fear of pain!"

The second day's shame ended, Romolino ordered Savonarola to appear next day to receive his sentence. A little before sunset that evening the bishops and others convened to consider what this

sentence should be. Consider? There was not
one moment's deliberation. Upon Savonarola and
Salvestro sentence of death was immediately resolved. One of the bishops suggested that Domenico might be spared. " No," answered his aids,
"letting him live will perpetuate the doctrines of
his master." " Then," replied the bishop—Romolino—"let him die. One friar, more or less, is of
small consequence."

That night, in his cell, each prisoner was informed of his sentence. Upon each the effect was
very different. Salvestro was greatly moved. Not
so was Domenico. To him it was simply glad tidings. Immediately he wrote the friars of San Marco
a noble letter, closing with the words: "Kiss all
the brethren for me. Collect all the works of Fra
Girolamo that are in my cell. Get them bound.
Place one copy in the library, and one in the refectory, to be read at table; let it be fixed by a chain,
so that the lay brethren may there sometimes read
it." So free of all fear was he that, when informed
that their bodies were to be burned after death, he
begged to be burned alive, that he might endure
the painful martyrdom for Jesus Christ's sake.

When the messenger entered Savonarola's cell,
he was engaged in prayer. On his knees, he listened to the reading of the sentence, and manifested
no emotion. Later, when supper was brought him,
he declined it, saying, "My mind needs support,
not my body." Soon after, a Benedictine monk
entered and performed for him the final rites of the
church. Barely had he departed, when the tender
Jacopo Nicolini, clad in black, a black hood drawn
close about his face, stepped within the cell. In-
quiring of Savonarola what service he could render
him, Savonarola begged he would obtain permission
for himself and his two friends to meet once more,

before they suffered. Nicolini quickly consented. The Seignory hesitated, but finally offered the great hall of the Five Hundred for the meeting.

It was far into the night when the three came together. They had not met since the evening of Palm Sunday. They had experienced forty days of confinement and suffering. They looked into each other's faces. What inroads had torture made upon their features! They grasped hands warmly. Few words were spoken. But one glance into the face of Savonarola assured his brethren that he had not denied himself. In the old manner Savonarola turned to Domenico, and said: "You want to be burned alive; but that is wrong. Do we yet know with what firmness we shall suffer even that to which we are condemned? That does not depend upon ourselves. It will be given us by the grace of God."

Then to Salvestro he gravely said: "I know that you are anxious to declare your innocence before the people. I admonish you to lay aside that thought, and to follow the example of our Lord Jesus Christ, who, even on the cross, would not justify himself."

Before separating, the two friars knelt before their superior, and for the last time received his benediction. Then sadly each returned to his cell. Savonarola slept some, his head resting on Nicolini's shoulder. Several times a smile lighted up his face, showing that his unconscious thoughts were not of the morrow. Before dawn he was engaged in prayer.

Once more, together, early in the morning, the three men partook of the sacrament. As Savonarola raised the host, he prayed, saying: "Lord, I know that thou art that perfect Trinity, invisible, distinct, Father, Son, and Holy Ghost. I know thou art the Eternal Word; that thou didst descend from heaven; that thou didst hang upon the cross to shed thy blood for our sins. I pray thee, that by that blood I may have remission of my sins, thy forgiveness for every offense against this city, for every sin of which I have, unconsciously, been guilty."

Almost immediately they were informed that the executioners were ready.

On the marble terrace, almost in the shadow of the great Duomo, stood three imposing tribunals, one to be occupied by the bishop who was to degrade the prisoners, another by the papal commissioners, the third by the Council of Eight, which was to pronounce the sentence of death. In front of these, on the very spot where but a short time before had blazed the vast bonfire of vanities, exactly where the ordeal by fire was to have taken place, extended a long, narrow platform out upon the plaza. At its end was erected an upright stake with a long cross-bar near the top, upon which the prisoners were to be suspended. At the foot of this cross lay an enormous pile of combustible material, ready for the ceremony of burning. Not until ten o'clock did Savonarola and his friends enter the scene. At the foot of the stairs of the palazzo publico, a Dominican monk removed the garments of their order. Not expecting this, and deeply moved, Savonarola exclaimed as he laid his robe in the hand of the man: "O holy robe! how much I have loved thee! Thou wast granted to me by the grace of God. To this hour I have preserved thee stainless. Now thou art taken from me. I do not give thee up."

In thin woolen garments, with feet bare and hands fastened behind them, they passed on to the first tribunal. There sat the Bishop of Vasona, once the pupil and friend of Savonarola. Taking his former teacher by the arm, the miserable bishop said, forgetting in his agitation the prescribed form of words, "I separate thee from the church militant and triumphant." "Militant, *not triumphant*," corrected Savonarola, steadfast in his hope, even in that darkest hour.

At the second tribunal the victims were delivered by the papal commissioners into the hand of the secular power, and so passed on to where stood Dolfo Spini as one of the Council of Eight. The sentence of death having been read, the monks with firm step walked along that narrow way, which ended at the ghastly cross-bar. "Yells of execration, cries as from throats thirsting for blood," rose around them as they neared the end. Even timid Salvestro was now full of courage. Domenico followed him, chanting the Te Deum. Then came Savonarola. To words of comfort offered him by a few among the dense ranks, he replied, "In the hour of death God alone can give comfort." To one who specially inquired what supported him in that last mortal hour, he answered, "Our Lord suffered as much for me." These were his last words before he reached the scaffold.

Salvestro first yielded up his life, saying, "Into thy hands I commit my spirit." Then Domenico stepped forward, his face beaming with joyful hope, and was suspended at the other end of the cross-bar. Before Savonarola's moment came, he took one long, steady look at the greedy multitude. Day after day in the great Duomo, hundreds of them had heard the gospel message from his lips. One can almost see his thoughts as he surveyed them. Where was the fruit of all his earnest teaching of righteousness? Was his beloved Florence any better for his having lived in it? Had truth taken any hold?

His hour having come, with great composure he "committed his soul to Christ," and placed himself in the hands of the executioner.

Their lives ended, the pile was lighted, and at dusk the ashes of the martyrs were gathered up, carried to the Ponte Vecchio, and thrown into the Arno. But before this last step, many of the devoted Piagnoni—among them several women of high rank, disguised as servants—made their way to the ever-to-be-memorable spot, and gathered up some of the ashes of Savonarola, who suffered May 23, 1498, four months before he had reached forty-seven years. Thus was the one great light of the fifteenth century suddenly extinguished, leaving Europe in great moral darkness until Martin Luther appeared on the scene.